BOARDLAND

Boardland
Copyright © 2018 by Tim Tweedie

Credits

Cover art & illustrations © by Carol David

Map of Boardland © by Tim Tweedie

All rights reserved. No part of this work may be reproduced or used in any form by any means—graphic, electronic, or mechanical including photocopying, without the written permission of the author

This is a work of fiction. Names, characters, incidents are either the product of the author's imagination or used fictitiously. Otherwise any resemblance to actual events, locations or persons, living or dead, is coincidental.

LCN 2018935066
ISBN 978-1-945539-20-6

BOARDLAND

By

Tim Tweedie

With Illustrations by
Carol David

Dunecrest Press

This book is dedicated to my six exceptional grandkids: Nicholas, Jonathan, Mikaia, Tyler, Kensie, and Sydney.

Also, a special thanks to my brother, Jim, for helping me put it all together.

Contents

Chapter 1	Forgotten, Again	1
Chapter 2	Boardland	19
Chapter 3	Mr. Abe and the Legend	45
Chapter 4	Spring and the Map	67
Chapter 5	The Tunnelers and the General	83
Chapter 6	Swoop and Special Powers	101
Chapter 7	Abstractshire and Primitivepality	127
Chapter 8	Rockbound Valley	153
Chapter 9	No Escape, But Chalk Power	173
Chapter 10	Trapped and Other Surprises	197
Chapter 11	The Plan	221
Chapter 12	The Battle	237
Chapter 13	Answers	261
Chapter 14	Manny and a Dream	273

Chapter One

Forgotten, Again

For a moment there was silence, probably one of the few times in any given day when there wasn't some form of frustration or tears. Then it happened.

"It isn't fair! I'm always the one expected to wash the dishes and clean up! Why is that, Mom?"

"Because I said so, that's why! You're my oldest daughter, Nadie, ten years old now, and therefore have many responsibilities around here. We've talked about this before. You know what I expect. What are you trying to do, ruin my night out with Garth?"

"Oh, now this one's name is Garth?"

"You better watch your mouth young lady or there'll be consequences. You know my new boyfriend's name, and you'll be nice to him when he picks me up."

There hadn't always been constant tension between Nadie and her brother and sister with their mother. Nadie could remember family times when their mother was there for them. Their father, David

Talbot, had always cared for their needs when he was home. Around the time Nadie's younger sister, Carona, learned to walk, their mother changed. She blamed everyone for stopping her from having the kind of life she wanted and harassed their father so much that she finally drove him away.

"Where are you and Garth going tonight, Mommy? I hope you're going to see that new movie about the toys that talk," Carona asked, trying as usual to calm things down.

"And you Carona, better have your room cleaned up and have studied your spelling words for the test tomorrow that Mrs. Durham sent that note about. I don't want to have to waste my time going to school again."

"Yes, Mommy. I just hope that Nadie or Caleb will have time to help me with them."

"Of course, they will. They know they have to. Besides, I'm going out and you know how bad I am at that kind of stuff."

"I don't think I'll have any time to help her because of all my homework and chores," a sobbing Nadie, exclaimed, pulling tissue from a handy box next to her.

As an artist and illustrator for books, their father hadn't been able to give them the luxurious life their mother felt she deserved, especially after sacrificing herself to give him three children. Yet, their father had always provided for them and still did, even though the divorce had been finalized five years earlier.

"Then I'm sure your brother, Caleb, will be more than happy to help."

"Happy to help with what?" they heard a deeper voice ask from the kitchen as Caleb entered the room.

"Help me with my spelling test for tomorrow," Carona replied with the pleading yet hopeful little smile she often used to gain support from whomever she could.

"Mom, you know I'm supposed to go over to Rich's tonight to work on that science project we're doing for Mr. Sears' class."

"As I understand it, that project is not due for a couple of weeks. You'll simply have to call him and tell him something came up and you can't make it. You're the oldest. Since I'm going out, you'll need to stay home anyway."

"We've only been able to get together twice. Can't you stay home once in a while?"

"How often I go out is my business and you'll do what I tell you. Besides, Garth could be the right one and you wouldn't want me to miss out on a chance of finding you a new father, would you?"

At the divorce hearing their mother received joint custody of the three of them, even though she tried to make their father look bad because his work kept him away so much. He needed to take a job wherever it was and right now most illustration work was in either Europe or the Far East. He loved his children and they returned his love. Their mother decided that for their "best interest" she would cut any communication between them that she could. Any letter or phone calls she retrieved from him for them disappeared.

Blotting her eyes with tissue, Nadia, who was still not sure if she'd rather keep crying or become angrier, exclaimed, "The father we have is perfect, and if you'd only realized that, you wouldn't have driven him away. Now you're trying to blame us for not helping you find a new one? We don't want a new one!"

"See, it's always about you. What about me and my happiness? I'm the one that's hurting here. I'm the one who has to deal with the three of you and give up so much. I need to look out for myself too!"

"You've always done a good job of that, Mom," Caleb quickly added.

"How dare you say that to me, when I get home I'll..."

A loud banging at the front door immediately turned Ginger Talbot's anger to smiles.

"That would be Garth for me," she sang.

Her voice became softer and melodic as she hurried towards the door.

"Hi, Garth, I've looked forward to this all day."

Standing at the door was a short, stout man who seemed to have lost his neck between his wide shoulders. His brown hair hung over his forehead like a puppy almost hiding his eyes. Ginger reached up and tenderly pushed the hair back from his face. "You don't want to hide those baby blues from me, do you? Oh, you have met the gang before, haven't you?"

It seemed to take Garth a moment to process Ginger's question. "Yeah, hi guys," he managed to say without any help as he gave a slight wave.

"We'd better be off, after all I don't want you to get me home as late as the last time we were out. Remember kids, tomorrow's Thursday, so I'm driving you to Aunt Molly's after school," Ginger yelled as she smiled and quickly closed the door.

The atmosphere in the room immediately changed. It was as though a dark cloud had lifted and the sun had come out making everything seem warm and bright again.

Nadia let out a deep sigh. "I guess I'd better get things cleaned up so I can do my homework."

"Since I can't get together with Rick, I've got plenty of time to help you with your spelling, Carona," Caleb said. He walked over and rubbed his little sister's blond hair for a moment as she beamed up at him. "Thanks, Caleb, I knew you'd help me."

"Sooner or later we always do, Carona, you know that. We have to stick together until Father comes back."

"Do you really think he's coming back, Caleb, like he says?" Nadia asked.

"You know he is. We just have to survive with Mom till he does."

"I don't think Mom really hates us," Carona added. "I just think she likes herself a lot more."

"If you ask me, we'd be better off if we could take care of ourselves without having a grown-up like her around."

"I'd have to agree with you, Nadie. I wish we could all get away from her. If I were only eighteen then I could take care of both of you and we could live without her."

"Or," Carona added, "until Father comes home from Europe or wherever he is. Isn't that right, Caleb?"

"The last time we e-mailed him he said he was illustrating books in Hong Kong for a new company. Just make sure you never show Mother how to e-mail. If she knew what we were doing we'd lose the computer."

"Caleb, where is Hong Kong?"

"Don't worry about it, Carona. It's part of a big country called China. By plane it's only half a day away, so he could be back for us at any time."

"Yeah, after he finishes drawing pictures for all those books," Carona added excitedly.

"An artist's job is never done," Caleb added.

"It's never done?" exclaimed Carona.

Nadia quickly stepped in, "Caleb meant that Father has a very creative and important job that takes a lot of time, but he'll be able to come home sometime soon and get us. That's what he meant."

"Yes, that's it, Carona, and then we'll be together with Father."

Caleb had been the one who held them together. He'd always thought things through and figured out the best direction to take. Once in a while he plowed forward too fast, having faith that his decisions were right and would turn out no matter what. Mostly he was right, which wasn't bad for a thirteen-year old who just started junior high school. Sometimes there were repercussions, like when he decided to pop a bully in the nose who'd kept harassing them about not having a father and having a mother who didn't care. But those weren't the exact words the bully used. His mother was very upset with Caleb, not because he hit someone, but because she was forced to come to school and conference with the principal. Caleb, who was tall and strong for his age, stood his ground. Although he did decide to apologize, he felt his decision had been necessary, especially since the bully stayed away from the three of them from then on.

Like Caleb, Nadie, an eleven-year-old sixth grader, was mature for her age. Growing up in a household undergoing constant discord and turmoil put her in the situation of being the 'mother' that Carona seldom had. She learned to take the lead with the household chores even though she resented being constantly dumped on her by their mother. Yet she was a realist. She knew she couldn't change the situation so she might as well adjust. Thanks to her mother, she understood the hardships of life but still believed things would get better. Her dark hair and eyes added to her striking appearance, and her humble disposition helped her to have many friends at school. She knew she was pretty, but never tried to use it to her advantage.

Carona was very friendly and always saw the best in everyone. She was noticeably shorter than most of her fourth grade classmates, but like her sister, she still stood out.

Carona's blond hair, deep blue eyes, round dimpled face, and positive attitude drew the attention of her classmates. She struggled in school since she often seemed to be day dreaming about something other than the subject being studied. It's not that she was below average. Her test scores were way above normal. It's just that her thoughts seemed to take her to different and magical places. In her mind she preferred picking wildflowers rather than working on her math assignment.

In the morning each of the youngsters got ready for school quietly so they wouldn't wake their mother. They'd all heard her come in late but pretended to be asleep. Less contact meant fewer problems.

Nadie, again, had made their lunches the night before which they quickly grabbed from the refrigerator as they hurried out to catch the school bus. They all looked forward to school and a chance to get out away from home. They were also glad they could still ride the same bus together when Caleb moved to the seventh grade and Valley Junior High School. Fortunately, the junior high was just across the park from Sutter Heights Elementary School. After school Caleb would walk back to Sutter Heights and ride home with his sisters. However, on Thursdays their mother would pick them up and take them over to her sister's house. Aunt Molly and their mother didn't really get along, but since Molly gave Caleb and Nadie free piano lessons and all of them a home cooked meal, their mother allowed it, as she said, 'for the sake of the kids'.

"How are you doing, Caleb?" Nadie asked as he jogged up beside her and Carona while they stood looking back at the school from the school parking lot.

"Okay," he managed to reply, obviously out of breath, "although Mr. Sears and Rick were upset with me for not working on the science project last night. Mr. Sears says we need all the time we can get if we want to complete a project worthy of a passing grade."

"What did you say?" a concerned Carona asked. "Did you tell him about Mom not letting you go to Rich's?"

"That wouldn't have done any good. It just would have made our family look more dysfunctional, so I just shrugged."

"What's 'dysfunctional?'" a puzzled Carona asked.

Nadie, looking disgusted, quickly answered, "It basically means messed up."

"Oh, then I guess it's good you didn't say anything, Caleb," Carona replied as she took a step forward and looked down the street. "I wonder where Mother is. We are supposed to go to Aunt Molly's today, aren't we?"

"Yep, that's what she said," Caleb replied as he searched in both directions for their car.

"Did you three miss the bus today?" they heard someone ask.

When they turned they saw Ms. Martinez, the Principal, smiling at them expectantly. She had been their principal for the last three years. All the students at Sutter Heights liked her. She was probably shorter and a little younger that most principals, but everyone knew she loved the students and her job. Since she'd met with their mother several times over the years, she was aware of, as she'd say, some of the challenges they faced.

"Hi, Ms. Martinez. No, we always catch the bus on time. None of us like the three-mile walk home," Caleb hastily replied. "On Thursdays, Mom's supposed to pick us up and take us to our aunt's."

"That's right. As I remember she's forgotten a couple times before."

"A couple," Nadie said as she shook her head back and forth not quite believing it had happened again. "Last time she was half an hour late!"

"As before, you're welcome to wait by my office while I call to remind her. She's probably just lost track of time. I know how that is."

"We'd appreciate that, Ms. Martinez," an embarrassed Nadie replied as they followed her back into the school.

Their family knew Sutter Heights Elementary School well. Not only were Nadie and Carona still attending, but Caleb had just graduated the year before. Before that, their father had also attended Sutter, although the school district had added more classrooms since David Talbot studied there. Even their mother briefly attended Sutter before her parents put her in a nearby private school, "for her own good", they had said. None of them knew what that had meant when their mother told them. Since her family had always been a bit snobby, Caleb figured they probably felt that Sutter Heights, as a public school, wasn't good enough from them.

As Ms. Martinez emerged from her office she told them that she'd gotten a hold of their mother. Apparently, she'd 'been delayed' but would be there within the hour.

"Within the hour?" Nadie couldn't help but shout out.

"Don't worry, Nadie. I told her I had office work to do and would gladly wait with you until she arrived."

"Thanks, Ms. Martinez, but that's not really fair to you," noted Carona.

"That's all right. I really do have school things I have to catch up on. I'll tell you what, Carona, why don't you go next store to Room 7, Mrs. Durham's and your current classroom and wait there. I know how much you like to draw, so I'll send you down to the custodian's office to get some chalk. You can all spend a little down time drawing while you wait."

That's really nice of you," replied Nadie, "but I still can't believe she forgot us...again!"

"I'll call Manny and tell him you're coming by to pick up some chalk. I'll let you know when your mom arrives."

"Are we that easy to forget?" a still frustrated Nadie asked as she looked at Caleb.

"Apparently," he replied as they walked past Room 7 and turned the corner towards Manny's office.

"Well, well, if we don't have the three Talbots at one time. Haven't seen you all together since last year. Caleb, you're looking more like your father every day. And you two beauties, if I were only a young man again, my, my."

"Good to see you again too, Mr. Manny," Caleb replied.

"You know better than that. It's just 'Manny' to you. Mister is something you say to someone important to show respect. Friends you call by their first name. After all, I knew your dad when he was only six, and have watched the three of you grow up too."

"If nothing else goes right we know you'll always be here for us and everyone else Manny," Caleb replied as he shook Manny's outstretched hand.

"Now a little bird told me the three of you need some chalk with which you're liable to draw masterpieces on the blackboard in Room 7. Is that true?" Manny asked with a big grin.

"I don't know about a little bird but I do know a nice principal who might have made that call," noted Nadie.

"To me they're both the same. That little bird calls me all day long and I can't wait to feed it. Whatever she wants Manny's more than happy to do. Now, I believe I have exactly what you need. Where did I put...oh yes, way up here," Manny said as he took three steps up a ladder leaning against the wall. "The corner of the top shelf, as I recall," he continued as he brought down three small boxes. "There aren't a lot of colors in these boxes, just the most important ones."

Manny, immediately gained Carona's full attention, "Colored chalk with the most important ones?" she asked inquisitively.

"Yes, just seven colors, the seven colors of the rainbow."

"Of the rainbow?" Carona repeated.

"Sure. Whenever you see a good strong rainbow you see these seven colors. You'd see the same colors if you held up a crystal or prism to the light. Just like the one the first teacher, Ms. Colton, hung up in Room 7 the first day the school opened. That's still there. When a light beam is shown through a prism, that beam would be broken into these seven beautiful colors which would be the colors of a spectrum. The same colors are always in a rainbow, red, orange, yellow, green, blue, indigo and violet."

"I remember seeing the crystal hanging in Room 7 when I was there," Caleb remarked.

"What's indigo, Manny?" Carona asked.

"Why young lady, that's a dark blue or gray blue color. It's not my favorite color, but it looks just fine in a rainbow. Now I have a box for each of you. That way there won't be any arguing over who gets what color first. You'll each have your own rainbow!"

Manny was best friends with just about every student who'd ever attended Sutter Heights. He'd been the custodian as far back as anyone could remember. Some parents, who'd long ago attended the school, believed the school had actually been built around him. They all laughed and said that it couldn't have been built on a better foundation. It didn't take new kids long to see what they meant. Manny's strong, positive character and love for those he served was obvious to all. Caleb was surprised, as the first Talbot child to attend Sutter Heights, when Manny recognized him as a Talbot since he looked so much like his father. To put him at ease, Manny, with his incredible memory, told Caleb some things about his dad as a young student that made Caleb laugh and feel right at home.

"You're always so nice, Manny," Carona said as she took a box and headed towards the door. "I'll be thinking of you when I'm drawing."

"That's a nice thing to say, Carona," Manny replied. "Then draw something big and colorful for me, maybe even a rainbow. You never know when a great work of art will appear!"

Caleb and Nadie took their boxes and followed Carona down the hallway to Room 7. Just as they arrived Mrs. Durham walked out. She was a middle-aged lady with slightly graying hair. Although older than the average teacher at Sutter Heights, she seemed to have more energy than even the younger teachers. She'd transferred from another school a few years after their father graduated to middle school. She had a reputation of being very artistic. Her classroom was always brightly decorated with pictures and artwork to stimulate her students. Her students liked her and parents, over the years, always hoped their children would be in her fourth grade class. She didn't seem especially surprised to see the Talbots at her door.

"Hi Caleb, Nadie, and Carona. You're back so soon?"

"Yes, Mrs. Durham. Our mother forgot us again and Ms. Martinez said it would be all right if we waited in your room 'til she came. Manny even gave us each some colored chalk to draw with," Carona explained quickly.

"That's fine with me. Ms. Martinez just called to say you'd be coming. I'd planned to leave the door unlocked and the lights on. All I ask is that you erase whatever you draw before you go, turn the lights out, and pull the door shut so it will lock. I'll need to put the class schedule and instructions on the blackboard first thing tomorrow morning. By the way, Carona, great job on the spelling test today."

"Thanks," a blushing Carona replied.

"We'll do exactly as you ask, Mrs. Durham. Thank you for letting us use your room," Caleb added.

"The three of you have a great evening!" Mrs. Durham exclaimed as she headed toward the parking lot.

"It's strange that we've all had classes in Room 7," Nadie mentioned as they walked towards the front of the room.

"Actually, the four of us," Caleb interjected. "Remember, Manny told me that Father spent the fourth grade in this room too."

"That's right, but we had Mrs. Durham for a teacher," noted Carona, "and I like her very much."

"She was one of my favorite teachers too," shared Nadie, "very creative and caring. I liked it when she read to us and drew some of the people, and places on the board. It really made the story interesting."

"I don't know about you, but I'm going to draw something big and colorful just like Manny said," Carona excitedly exclaimed as she held the indigo chalk.

"And what would that be?" Nadie asked.

"I think I'll start with a big mountain with a lake next to it and a meadow full of wildflowers," Carona replied as an indigo mountain began to appear.

"That masterpiece might take up the whole blackboard," Caleb quipped with a grin.

"No, I'll just stay on this side. You and Nadie can have the rest."

"Then, I'm going to draw a beautiful house," Nadie said, "one that I hope the three of us, along with Father, will live in someday."

"And I'll draw my favorite raptors," Caleb added.

"Raptors? Nadie exclaimed in disgust. You're going to draw birds again, ones that eat other birds and animals?"

"Sure, birds of prey provide an important balance in nature and hawks and eagles rule the sky," Caleb replied as he immediately began sketching what appeared to be a sharp beak.

"I really don't understand why boys like things that eat other things. I do like the idea and freedom of flying wherever you want. I've often wished I could just fly away, but why not draw a robin or hummingbird?" Nadie shared without actually expecting an answer.

Chapter Two

Boardland

The three of them became lost in their drawings, giving them each a chance to forget for a while and create a world they'd like to be a part of. Soon the blackboard was covered with a tall mountain, lake, and flowered meadow as well as an early American two storied pillared house with window shutters and white lace curtains hanging in them. There were also two enormous eagles with menacing claws and beaks sitting in a tall Weeping Willow tree that Caleb had drawn right next to Nadie's house.

"That's a real nice mountain," Nadie exclaimed as she patted Carona on the back.

"Yeah, all you need now is to draw a big entrance to a cave on it. That way someone could live there or explore it!" Caleb added.

"You'd like that wouldn't you, Caleb, although it would be a good place to hide," Nadie replied, feeling a cave might not be a bad idea.

"Then we could all live there by the lake and meadow!" Carona replied with a grin as she stretched and drew a large upside-down U on her mountain.

"Now it's perfect!" Caleb exclaimed.

"No, not quite," Carona added. "I still need to add a beautiful rainbow over the top of my mountain just for Manny. After all, he did give us the seven colors of a rainbow. It wouldn't be right if I didn't draw one."

"Good idea," Nadie replied as she began to put her chalk back into its box.

With Caleb lifting her up just high enough, Carona carefully arched a big thick line of each color on the side of her mountain. As he put her down and stepped back to look at her work, a very pleased Carona said, "Now it's perfect!"

Outside the classroom window Caleb noted that the sun was low in the sky. It was beaming into the room and hitting the blackboard drawings with a rainbow from the crystal prism that had been hanging near them for years. It had been an hour and their mother still hadn't arrived.

"Look! My rainbow is bright and glowing!" Carona reported as they all saw how beautiful it was with the light from the prism resting on it.

"Hey, a light beam is focused right on the cave too. It's as though you can almost see into it," Caleb said as he moved forward for a closer look. "Nadie, does that light beam look like it's dancing around inside the cave, or am I losing my mind?"

Nadie also moved closer to the board. "It looks like it's dancing to me too."

"Are either of you singing?" Carona asked.

Caleb and Nadie looked around at Carona and they both shook their heads no.

"Why do you ask?" Nadie replied.

"I hear singing and it sounds like its saying "there is always a flicker of hope" or something like that."

"It's saying what?" Caleb asked.

"I hear it now too," Nadie exclaimed as she moved even closer to the blackboard and the mountain picture Carona had drawn. "It sounds like it's...it's...coming from the cave!"

They all stepped as close as they could to the board and put an ear towards the cave.

"I hear it now!" Caleb shouted. "It's the light beam that's flickering. It seems to be dancing and singing, 'there is always a flicker of hope no matter what the situation...all you need to do is follow the rainbow'!"

"I can't believe it!" Nadie exclaimed. "I hear the same thing...the light beam in the cave is dancing and singing...no way!"

"What should we do?" Carona asked.

"I think we all must be going crazy. Maybe we need food, or maybe it's something we already ate. What did you put in our sandwiches last night, Nadie?" Caleb asked.

"Nothing I haven't put in them a hundred times before", she replied while attentively listening to the song coming from the cave.

As they watched and listened, the flickering light in the cave seemed to get bigger and closer until it filled the opening of the cave as it danced and sang. Then suddenly it stopped. The three of them couldn't believe their eyes and ears.

"Why don't you come on in? It's your picture after all," they heard a melodic voice ask.

"Did you hear that, Nadie?" Caleb yelled.

"I did!" replied an excited Carona.

"I'm afraid I did too!" Nadie added.

"The light beam...it has long white hair and bright red eyes...and they're looking right at me!" Caleb bleated out.

"So, are you going to answer me or not?" the voice asked.

There was a long pause as the three of them stood in awe of the talking light beam. Confusion, disbelief and amazement gripped them all at once. What should one say to a talking light beam they all wondered at the same time?

Finally, Caleb spoke up. "What...Who...are you?" he sputtered out.

"I'm Flicker, of course. I've been waiting for you", the voice replied.

"What do you mean 'you've been waiting for us'?" Nadie asked, still not sure if she wanted to talk to a light beam named Flicker.

"We actually thought you'd come visit us sooner, but we can't be right all the time," Flicker's melodic voice replied.

"Visit you?" Carona quickly asked.

"Sure, visit the world you just drew under the rainbow, a world of amazing things that all three of you are already a part of. You'll just have to visit to see," Flicker replied.

Caleb, still confused and not sure if he wanted any part of what he heard, decided to ask again, "What do you mean waiting for us?"

"You're all part of our history. The Legend says that you will one day visit us when we need you the most, and when the time is right, and now the time is right. To be exact, everything that was supposed to come together to bring you into our world has now happened."

"Like what has happened besides us listening to a singing light beam, in a picture, on a blackboard, in Room 7, that seems to now be talking to us?" Caleb asked. "If that doesn't sound whacky..."

"Perfect, so you do understand, although you did forget the chalk, prism, and the rainbow with the sun shining on it that brought me here... oh, and the fact that no one else is around."

"And you've been waiting for all those things to just happen...all at once...to the three of us?" Nadie asked inquisitively.

"Of course, everything happens for a reason at the right time, Nadie," Flicker replied.

"You know my sister's name?" Carona asked.

"Of course we know you, Carona, and Caleb. You three are the most important part."

"I'm still very confused about all of this. What kind of world are you talking about and why do you keep saying 'we?'" Nadie asked.

"Let me ask you this. Do you like the situation you're living in right now or would you rather visit a world you had a part in creating?"

"What kind of a world is it?" exclaimed Caleb.

"Well, to be exact, it's a world that exists beyond this very blackboard. You'll really have to see it to believe it! Like I said, it's quite amazing!"

"You mean we can actually visit this world and go through the blackboard?" Carona asked with delight.

"That's what I've been saying. There really isn't much time left. Everything is just right for you to visit Boardland, but in a few minutes, all the things that have made it possible will disappear. It's really a great opportunity for you, and I'd gladly show you around."

"Could we leave and come home when we wanted?" Nadie asked.

"When all things come together of course you could," Flicker said with a grin, "but we really don't have much time."

"I'm still quite confused by all this and still have a thousand questions," a cautious Nadie replied.

"I understand your concern and confusion, but we'll be able to answer your questions once we get to Boardland. Sometimes you just have to have faith that everything will turn out all right. Sometimes you just have to take that important first step to discover something new and different," Flicker melodically replied.

"I am concerned, but I'm also very intrigued. An adventure, a change from our current situation, after all, it is only a visit, isn't it Flicker?" Caleb asked. As usual Caleb was cautious about doing something new or different without knowing all the possibilities. Yet he also had an impulsive streak. Given the choice of an adventure or going home to an uncaring and manipulative mother, he eagerly made his decision.

"Of course," Flicker replied with another grin.

"Then I'm for it," Caleb declared. "What do I do?"

"It's all very complicated yet very simple at the same time. You just reach up with your hands, stretch and widen the opening of the cave under the rainbow and then crawl on in. That's it," Flicker replied.

Hesitating, Caleb asked, "But how can I get through a thick blackboard?"

"You mean we can actually visit this world and go through the blackboard?"

"Well, that's the complicated part. Do you know what osmosis is?" Flicker asked.

"I do," Nadie said as she quickly held up her hand, then blushed and just as quickly pulled it down realizing she wasn't still in class.

"Good, Nadie, then what is it?" Flicker replied.

"It's like in science when we studied how liquids pass in and out through plant membranes. It's how they can go through something almost solid without hurting it."

"You're as smart as I knew you were, and you're right! People are liquid since they're made mostly of water, so that allows you to pass through the osmotic gateway in the cave without even feeling it. It's a bit of the more complicated part of traveling to Boardland."

"I want to go with you, Caleb!" Carona shouted. "I love adventure. It will be wonderful and I'm sure Flicker will take good care of us."

"Then I guess I'll go along too," Nadie added. "Besides, I'll probably explode if I have one more night of cleaning and being yelled at by Mom. Boardland has got to be better than that."

"Then you need to reach up and stretch open the cave and follow each other through to Boardland," Flicker explained. Now only Caleb's behind could be seen sticking out of the blackboard.

As they crawled through the mountain cave, the opening grew larger until they all could stand up.

Flicker, with his light still blazing, led the way. There was a moist, then dry, warm and cozy feeling, like they'd just stepped out of a shower into a sunny warm room.

"Do you hear music, Nadie?" Carona asked.

Nadie paused for a moment, "I hear something but I'm not sure..."

"Where's my birthday cake? You told me it would be here by now!" yelled an angry, deep throaty voice. "I want my picture taken with my cake!"

"But General, you told me you wanted it to be part of the parade so all of Boardland could celebrate your birthday with you. You said, 'Let everyone have a day of celebration to revere their benevolent leader'," replied Captain Thumb.

"Yes, yes, how could I forget...my loyal subjects, they should be allowed to celebrate this day. All of Boardland should be reminded of their kind and glorious father's birthday! Of course I remember!" General Eraser shouted back.

"Then do you still want me to cancel the evening smudging patrols?" the Captain asked.

"The patrols, the patrols, of course not, for today is the perfect time to catch some Scribbles and the like. They will feel less threatened as they enjoy the gaiety of the parade and the holiday I've given them. Double the patrols! We still need to cleanse our land of all undesirables for the artistic purity of our beloved land. As usual I will take pleasure in making my evening rounds. Even on my birthday I will do my part to cleanse the land."

"Very well, my General, and I assure you that all your men will be here when your cake arrives to cheer their precious leader, that is, before they go on patrol," the Captain replied with a salute. "Yet, my dear General, I need to make you aware of another report of talk regarding the 'Legend'."

"Fantasy, pure fantasy," the General shouted out. "Just a fairy tale told by those few putrid drawings that blight our land. If there were any truth to it, I would know. Besides, who could possibly threaten my reign, I mean my command?"

"You're right, my General. Yet our spies still hear of it."

"Then it should disappear with the implementation of my plan for the final cleansing of the land," the General blurted back. "And have the patrols be extra vigilant this evening."

"Yes, my General. The parade and your cake should arrive in the hour. I'll get things ready for your picture," the Captain replied as he bowed and backed from the room.

By now the Talbots could all hear the music but had no idea where it was coming from. Suddenly, Caleb jumped into the air. "Man, what in the world was that?" he yelled.

"Was what?" Flicker replied.

"That thing that almost ran me over!"

Flicker turned and looked back down the cave. "Was it rather chunky, brown and furry?" he asked.

Caleb still looking behind him, "Yeah, but I could swear that it had a human face."

"Well then, that was just a Tunneler. They mostly stay underground since they like the dark. We don't see them very often. A bunch of them appeared in Boardland several years ago. If you ask me, someone went crazy with his chalk."

"Do they bite or anything?" Carona asked.

"Not that I know of so far," Flicker replied. "We'd better be on our way."

As Flicker's light began to dim, an opening in the tunnel in front of them became larger and brighter with the music becoming even louder. After a minute or two they emerged through a partially bush covered opening into a meadow near a blue lake on the other side of a large indigo colored mountain.

"Look! That's the meadow and lake I just drew on the chalkboard!" Carona exclaimed. "It is even full of my wildflowers!"

Nadie and Caleb couldn't believe what they were seeing. "Yes, yes," shouted Nadie. "It is your meadow and flowers."

"And the music is coming from the road in the meadow over there. It seems to be a band playing...in a parade?" Caleb sputtered.

"Yes, it must be a parade. I see the instruments...marching...but no one seems to be playing them!" Carona shouted as the music got louder.

"That's because they're playing themselves!" Nadie observed.

"Of course they're playing themselves. That's what the instruments you and your classmates drew on the blackboard do. All instruments are made to play," said Flicker. "I suggest we watch the parade from behind these rocks. For now, it's best we keep your visit just between us."

"Look, Nadie," Carona shouted. "That's the funny looking trombone that Mrs. Durham drew on the board last week when the music teacher came."

"Yes, the Creator did draw that one," Flicker shared softly.

"The one that keeps sliding way out like it's segmented?" Nadie replied.

"Yeah, and the big round drum with the four small drums inside of it, Billy drew that one." Carona excitedly replied.

"They do all look kind of weird, like they were drawn by fourth graders," Caleb observed. "But the saxophones look very real!"

"Yeah, the music teacher drew three of those," Carona explained.

"Look at that...Are those people marching behind them carrying banners and flags?" Nadie said as she tried to understand what exactly she was seeing.

"I don't know for sure." Caleb replied. "Some look like different colors of fuzzy people. Some look like stick people. Others look like bouncing springs with faces, and there is one of them with stick like arms and legs carrying an American flag that looks like a ball made up of the letter Q's...with a human face!"

"Oh, that's a Scribble," Flicker replied. "I'm surprised to see him in the parade."

"What's that way behind them?" asked Carona.

"Those are floats being pulled by trucks or horses of course," Flicker replied. "Don't most parades have them?" he asked.

"Usually," said Caleb, "but those trucks look like they're falling apart. One of them only has three wheels...and the horses look like they should have been sent to the glue factory years ago!"

"Everyone, you know, who draws on the blackboard isn't a Michelangelo. Most of the artists in Room 7 are in the fourth grade. Besides, people just draw things the way they see them the best they can. It's their ideas that are most important," Flicker shared.

Caleb, rubbing his brow, replied, "I guess you're right but this is really weird!"

"I see a big white, black and red striped birthday cake with a lot of candles on the back of that big truck," Carona said as she pointed to what appeared to be the end of the parade.

"Oh yes. That's the birthday cake for the General," Flicker shared. "He's sort of like our President."

"And what in the world are those things moving alongside the truck, Flicker?" a gasping Nadie exclaimed. "They look like walking fingers wearing red and black uniforms! The two at the end are carrying a large banner with some kind of picture on it."

"That they are, Nadie. Those are some of the General's soldiers watching over his birthday cake until they get to his residence near Realtown."

"He has fingers for soldiers?" she questioned.

"I'm afraid so, but that's another story. You are enjoying the gaiety of the parade, aren't you?" Flicker asked.

"In a strange sort of way, yes!" Caleb replied rubbing his brow again. As the banner came closer, he saw what looked like a large eraser with a mustached head and face pictured on it. "But I don't understand all this."

"It can be rather confusing for someone who wasn't drawn on the blackboard," Flicker replied.

Nadie also confused spoke up. "Let me get this right. Everything in Boardland was at one time drawn by somebody on the blackboard in Room 7?"

"Yes, very good. Boardland is a creation of all the students, and especially the Creator, who have drawn on the blackboard. That's why our world is called Boardland!"

"This is such a wonderful place!" Carona exclaimed. "And to think that I always believed that once we erased the board, everything we had drawn was gone."

"You'd be surprised to know how many things people do and say actually exist and remain out there somewhere," Flicker replied.

"That's a scary thought," Caleb shared. "Now just who is this Creator you're talking about?"

"Oh, for the last twenty years the Creator's personal name is Mrs. Durham."

"Mrs. Durham, my teacher?" Carona asked.

"Of course, she's the one that controls the blackboard in Room 7. She also does most of the drawing and writing herself, thereby, over the years, creating much of what exists in Boardland!"

"I'm even more confused," Nadie confessed. "How do all the things drawn on the board get...you know...through the board into Boardland? And, why would they?"

"Both good questions. They come through the board similar to the way you came through, by a special type of osmosis. Room 7 has a very unusual physical arrangement. During most of the day the sun shines on the blackboard causing it to warm up and become covered with a small amount of electricity from the sun. The sun is very amazing in what it can do. Even in Boardland our sun has unique powers. The sun's rays on the blackboard cause a small vibration or oscillation across its surface when the sun finally ceases to shine on it. That's when everything left on the board gradually passes through to Boardland. Isn't that fantastic?" Flicker exclaimed.

"I really like all this," Carona interjected. "Does Mrs. Durham know that she's the Creator?"

"Not that we're aware of. We just appreciate that she keeps expanding our world, otherwise we'd slowly disappear," Flicker replied as his voice trailed off.

"Disappear?" Caleb asked.

Flicker, seeming a bit uneasy, quickly replied, "I was just rambling, just thinking out loud, nothing to worry about."

"What is that?" Carona asked as she looked down the road. "Can you hear it?"

"I do!" Nadie exclaimed. "It looks like a long sentence of words and they seem to be running together and chanting, 'I will not talk in class...I will not talk in class,' over and over again!"

"That's just a sentence passing by. It will be gone in a moment," Flicker explained.

"Yeah, but how, why...?" Caleb started to ask.

"Oh, I know what you're asking. Words can live on in Boardland too, although all they can do is repeat what they say. They don't have much of a personality. The Creator often has students who sometimes need a reminder about following the class rules write them on the board."

"I know! Mrs. Durham makes us write the rules several times when we don't follow them. I had to do that last week when I forgot to throw my gum away when I came back into the classroom," Carona shared as her face turned slightly red.

Nadie was staring up into the sky, her mouth slightly open. "What is that Flicker? It's sure beautiful."

"That glowing light floating down towards us?" Flicker asked.

"Yeah," she replied.

"That's my friend, Gleam. She does make you want to smile, doesn't she?"

Caleb, whose attention was also drawn to the soft white oval light sputtered, "She has the face of an angel."

"She has the same effect on me," Flicker sighed.

"Flicker, who are your new friends? They're so real they must be the Talbots we've so long expected," a warm and comforting voice asked.

Flicker, hesitating for a moment, replied, "As usual, Gleam, you're right. The Talbots just arrived. We've been enjoying the General's birthday parade together."

"Wow, who drew her?" Caleb found himself asking.

"Actually, several of us in Boardland were created when the first sun was chalked onto the new blackboard when Room 7 was equipped," Caleb heard the comforting voice of Gleam explain. "All the suns that have ever been drawn on the board have been absorbed into our one sun, the Great Illuminator. He's the one that created us sunbeams and rays. We all work for him. He shines his light by day, and then rests after the lights have been turned off in Room 7, for yours and our night."

"You both work for him?" Carona asked.

"Yes," Gleam continued, "We watch over all the sketches and drawings in Boardland by day, especially those most vulnerable, the Scribbles and Scrawls. The Illuminator feels everyone's artistic ideas that have ever been drawn on the blackboard have a right to exist. They may not look very real, like the Scribbles and Scrawls, or be near perfect sketches or drawings, but they all have value and should be allowed to exist in Boardland.

"Why do you need to look after them?" a concerned Carona asked.

Gleam looked inquisitively at Flicker and asked, "Then you haven't told them yet about the Legend?"

"Uhh, not all of it, I was just showing them around and then the parade appeared. Since they just arrived I didn't want to overwhelm them with, ah, too much information," Flicker explained.

"You may be right about that," Gleam replied. "In answer to your question, Carona, some drawings just need a little more nurturing than others. Just like some people need a little more support because of their differences."

"I think I understand," Carona replied with a smile. "I have a friend who is blind. I have lunch with her and help her to some of her classes. She really appreciates my friendship."

"Yes, Carona, it is something like that," Gleam replied. "By the way, Flicker, it will be getting dark soon. The sun will disappear from the window in Room 7 and the Great Illuminator will extinguish his light for the day. You'd better find a safe, I mean comfortable place for the Talbots to spend the night."

"With all the excitement of seeing them I almost forgot. We need to be moving further along into Boardland. I've never had guests like the Talbots, before. Where should I take them?"

"Since you can go anywhere, take them to Realtown. I'm sure they'll feel most comfortable there," Gleam replied.

"That would be the best place. They should probably stay with Mr. Abe. He would take good care of them," Flicker noted.

"Then you'd better be on your way," Gleam suggested. "I feel the warm rays of the Illuminator being reabsorbed."

"Everyone, to Realtown and Mr. Abe's," replied Flicker while Gleam smiled and waved as she floated into the sky towards the Illuminator.

"This is a very strange and different place, Flicker, but I'm still trying to figure it out and understand why we're here," Caleb admitted.

Flicker smiled as he started walking towards the road in the direction the parade had taken. "We all hope you'll find your time here enlightening."

As Caleb began walking towards Realtown he felt a strange sensation. Walking seemed almost effortless to him as though he could keep going forever. He had to hold himself back from passing Flicker who himself was moving along briskly.

Carona skipped merrily along at the back of the group, stopping occasionally to pick one of the chalky wildflowers she'd drawn earlier. Nadie also had no trouble keeping up. She appeared to be apprehensive about their journey, especially as they left Carona's primitive drawing and headed towards a distant village whose buildings looked a lot like an actual town.

Caleb was enthralled by just about everything. He walked along next to Flicker looking everywhere at once and just about stepped on a little creature that looked like a cross between a squirrel and a rabbit.

"Hey fella, watch where you're putting your feet. Just because you're more real than I am doesn't mean you can squash me. Even the Fingers leave me alone," the creature yelled as he ran into a forest of purple shrubs.

"That thing talks too?" an astounded Caleb asked.

Flicker spoke, trying to suppress a smile, "Of course, and by the way, we call him, Squirrelbit. Only the person who drew him knows exactly what he's supposed to be. As to his being able to talk, just about anything that moves, or has arms and legs in Boardland can talk. Artists often say that their art gives them a voice with which to speak to others. I guess in turn the things they draw, their art, continue to speak for them...and themselves."

"Weird, but that's pretty consistent with everything else here," Caleb replied as he looked up. "Hey, look at those houses, Nadie, they are nearly perfect but they each are so different."

"The buildings look like something you'd find in a real town, but nothing seems to match. One house is a Victorian and another is early American colonial...and there are some basic L shaped ranch styles...and look, those people, they look almost like us!" she exclaimed.

"Yes, those people are almost as perfect as you. That's why they live in Realtown where everything has been drawn by excellent artists, many by the Creator herself," Flicker proudly shared. "However, it is our smallest community since most of the people and buildings in Boardland have been drawn by fourth graders."

"There are other communities in Boardland besides Realtown?" Carona asked as she bent down to pet a white and black Border Collie that had just run up to her.

"Of course," Flicker replied, as he paused for a moment as though he was trying to decide what else he should say. "The General, who considers himself a master art critic, has organized Boardland into communities based upon the artistic merit of each piece of art drawn on the blackboard. So besides Realtown, which is based upon artistic realism, we have Impressionville for impressionist art, Primitivepality for art considered primitive or naïve, and Abstractshire for art which let's say is more modern and abstract."

"Wow, your General must be very knowledgeable," Nadie replied.

"Thanks for rubbing my back, little girl," a gravelly voice said. The Border Collie ran back towards a large Victorian, while Carona clapped some black and white chalk dust from her hands.

Carona looked a bit surprised.

"I guess I should have known he'd be chalky and could talk, but it still surprises me that he does," she said while watching the collie run into a large yellow and brown Victorian.

While they walked down the streets of Realtown they noticed how perfect every drawing looked. From the colorful gardens, to the beautiful flowing willow and aspen trees, and the white picket fences, everything was in its place looking like a flawless painting by a master artist. Occasionally they'd pass a person who'd smile then hurry on by. Others, seeing the four of them approach, would leave their porches and go inside. Several times Nadie noticed children peering out a window. Caleb smiled back but found he was more and more apprehensive about the whole visit. Carona continued to skip, wave and greet everyone with a "good evening", even though no one returned her salutations. Flicker guarded, but always polite and positive, led them to a large early American Colonial home which took up a large cul-de-sac just off what a street sign said was Lovely Lane.

"Wow!" Nadie exclaimed, "Is this where we're going to spend the night?"

Flicker paused and turned towards the Talbots. "Yes, isn't it a lovely home?"

"Is this where Mr. Abe lives?" asked Nadie.

Flicker grinned and replied, "It is, but let me tell you a little about Mr. Abe. He is very popular in Boardland. He's also one of our earliest citizens. I'm sure you'll come across other drawings of him as you travel since many people have chalked his face on the blackboard. This 'Mr. Abe' is the best artistic rendition of him. Even the General is careful with him, I mean holds him in ah... high esteem."

"We're not talking about Abraham Lincoln, are we?" Caleb asked.

"Why yes, Caleb, we are. Wasn't he one of your greatest Presidents with his picture hung in many classrooms?"

"Yes, but he was real!" expressed Caleb.

"True," Flicker replied, "but I think you'll find that here he is also very real and that this Mr. Abe is very much like him."

Chapter Three

Mr. Abe and the Legend

They approached Mr. Abe's double white doors and waited while Flicker knocked and white chalk wafted from the doors. Something moving in the tall sword ferns on the right side of the house drew Caleb's attention. He turned to see what it was but saw nothing. Within a moment a tall slender man wearing a tall black top hat along with a black coat with tails that hung just below his knees answered. He looked to be a man in his early fifties, obviously the President pictured before the aging ordeal of the Civil War. When the man saw who was at his front door he graciously tipped his hat and gave a slight bow. "Welcome to my humble abode. You must be the Talbots," he announced as he shook their hands and welcomed them each by name. "I've, I mean we've been looking forward to your visit. By all means will you please come in?"

Surprisingly enough, the inside of Mr. Abe's house displayed an early American décor. Someone had obviously chalked the interior based upon extensive research and study.

Caleb was the first to speak. "Mr. Abe, thank you for your welcome, although I'm still not sure how everyone seems to know who we are."

Laughing, Mr. Abe replied, "Please, all my friends just call me Abe, and as to knowing who you are, the three of you are too perfect to be drawings. Hasn't my friend, Flicker, told you about our Legend?"

Flicker, again looking a bit uncomfortable, quickly spoke, "I did tell them that they were part of our history and that the Legend said they would come to Boardland when the time was right. Beyond that, Mr. Abe, I wasn't sure if I should be the one to tell them the rest."

"I see," Abe replied as he stroked his beard in deep thought.

The silence was broken by a faint tapping on the window next to the fireplace. A curious expression appeared on Abe's face as he walked towards the sound, and then opened the window. Instantly a strange Scribble jumped in. Caleb figured that the Scribble must have been what he saw moving in the bushes outside.

"I'm sorry, Mr. Abe, but it was getting dark and I had nowhere else to go," the nervous Scribble reported. I'm afraid I've been a bit silly and over enthusiastic."

"Calm down, Curly. Why do you say that?" Abe asked.

"Because I decided to help my friends carry the American flag in the General's birthday parade earlier today and...and...I know it was stupid but...some Fingers saw me so I ran."

Nadie immediately recognized the Scribble. "Flicker, isn't that Q from the parade, the little curly Q character we saw?"

"Why yes, it is. I was afraid he'd be seen."

"I'm sorry for the interruption, my friends. It will just be a moment," Abe said as he turned back towards the Q. "Now Curly, were you followed?"

"No, I'm pretty sure I lost them when I ran through the bushes," he replied.

"Just relax then. You're welcome to spend the night. Flicker would you be so kind as to take Curly to the basement?"

Flicker nodded, "Yes," and then told Curly to follow him as they both left the room.

Caleb, his curiosity overcoming propriety, spoke, "What was that all about, if you don't mind my asking?"

"No, I don't mind. You actually should know. It has a lot to do with the Legend and why you are here. Please take a seat. May I offer you some tea?"

Carona immediately spoke up, "I would really like some hot tea please."

Mr. Abe smiled then rang a small bell that sat on the coffee table in front of him. Immediately, a small, round woman wearing a long-aproned dress and a drawn cloth bonnet appeared. Her features were hard to discern. She was obviously drawn by an artist whose style was impressionistic. Nadie couldn't help but stare.

"And this is my lovely wife, Mary Todd. Mary, I'd like to introduce our guests, the Talbots."

Mary looked carefully at each of them for a moment then turned to Abe. "I'm sure they'd all appreciate some tea. I'll be glad to make some."

"Thank you, Mary," Abe replied as she hurried out of the room.

"I have to apologize for the bell. Mary likes me to use it rather than calling for her. I'm sure you noticed that Mary isn't drawn to quite the same level of perfection as the rest of Realtown. Since she is my wife and the best drawing of herself to be completed on the blackboard, I'm allowed to have her with me. But even that privilege could be taken from me at any moment."

"Does that have something to do with your history and the Legend?" Carona asked.

"Very much so, let me explain. When Room 7 was built and the first class entered the room in 1965, Ms. Colton decorated her room and hung her favorite crystal in the window for luck, I guess. I was one of the first drawings placed upon the blackboard. I believe that was due to the fact that they opened the school in the middle of the school year in February around my birthday. To my surprise I found myself in this strange world of darkness. Fortunately, immediately following the drawing of me, the first Creator, Ms. Colton of course, drew a big smiling sun on the board welcoming her class. That's when Boardland came to life. The Sun in Boardland absorbed the reflected light both from your sun and the classroom lights. Upon seeing a flash of light that appeared to be a rainbow, I went into the blackboard and appeared in Boardland the next morning. I was both scared and surprised! The first thing I saw was the bright sun and a girl who looked like the rainbow. As time went on more and more drawings appeared early each morning, Boardland became a very chaotic place. Strange looking drawings, mountains, buildings, numbers, letters, creatures and peoples of all shapes and sizes suddenly appeared.

"So, you were here when Boardland was first created?" Nadie asked.

"I believe I was. I'm still not completely sure how or why. But I was glad to be somewhere. As more and more drawings and writings arrived, I did my best to help create a town for the drawings that appeared in Boardland as I called it. All kinds of houses and buildings were drawn or sketched so our town grew.

Everyone lived together whether they were drawn as realism, impressionistic, primitive or abstract. I have to admit, we all got along very well all those years and helped each other adjust to our new world."

Carona, listening intently, exclaimed, "That must have been fun and rewarding, Mr. Abe. I mean, creating a new world where everyone got along."

"That it was, Carona, until someone drew a strange character that looked like a very large black eraser. The problem was it had a square mustached face and was drawn with what looked like some kind of military uniform. He called himself, 'General Eraser', and began throwing his weight around...literally."

"How did he do that?" Nadie asked.

"He was a large eraser, and everything in Boardland is made mostly of chalk. When he threw his weight around, he erased any drawing that got in his way or he felt wasn't drawn to perfection. Unfortunately, he considered himself to be the ultimate art critic."

"He actually destroyed drawings and...people and things not drawn to his satisfaction?" Caleb asked in disbelief.

I'm afraid so. That's when everything began to change in Boardland," Abe said with a sigh.

"Couldn't you and others stop him?" Nadie asked.

"Some of us tried, but he was an eraser so when he was grabbed he simply erased. It was really awful.

Then at about the same time someone began drawing picture of fingers on the blackboard."

Carona, looking a bit confused asked, "You mean like fingers from a hand?"

"Yes, don't ask me why but all kinds of fingers, large fingers, small pinky fingers, even thumbs. Some were almost perfect renditions of fingers while others were more primitively drawn. Unfortunately for us they were also drawn with arms, legs and faces."

"Like the ones we and Flicker saw in the parade today?" Caleb asked.

Just then Flicker entered the room. "Yes, yes, Caleb, just like the ones we saw guarding the General's cake," he interjected.

"Then the Talbots have seen some of the General's soldiers?" Abe asked.

"I'm sorry to say they have," Flicker replied.

"The fingers are his soldiers?" Caleb asked. "Why would he want fingers for soldiers?"

"We should have seen it coming, but then again up until the General's appearance in Boardland we only looked on the bright side of everything," Abe answered. "The General made the most real looking fingers into his officers, like Captain Thumb and Sergeant Tall One. Others fingers became his own personal soldiers."

"Were those two the most perfect of the drawings?" Carona asked.

"Yes, most perfect of the drawings and the best at...smudging," Abe said as he shook his head and looked down.

"Smudging?" Caleb exclaimed, "You mean they smeared or rubbed out other drawings?"

"Captain Thumb was most effective at it. During the day, while on patrol, he'd identify any drawing that wasn't up to the General's standards. He'd smudge them and leave them for the General who'd move around in the early evening and completely erase or as he says, 'cleanse Boardland of all undesirables'. The Fingers made perfect soldiers for him."

"Then the General became a dictator and Boardland became an autocracy that, I guess you'd say, killed or destroyed people, I mean drawings of people and things?" Caleb asked excitedly.

"That's exactly what he and his soldiers did. Then he divided all of us into different groups based upon our artistic qualities. He'd evaluate everything and everyone down to their size, color, and shape, determining how well they matched their real counterparts. Then he'd assign them to a town, a town they weren't supposed to leave except on special occasions."

"You mean Realtown, Impressionville, Primitivepality and Abstractshire?" Carona asked.

"Why yes, how'd you..."at that point Flicker interrupted. "Mr. Abe, I did tell them the names of our different towns."

"Then, Carona, you have an exceptional memory," Mr. Abe replied.

"So, everyone is actually a prisoner in the town they're assigned to and at any time could be smudged by a Finger and then erased by the General?" Caleb asked.

"That's what's become of Boardland. Most everyone lives in fear. That's where the Legend comes in," Mr. Abe replied.

Mr. Abe's story had brought Carona to tears, "I can't believe this is happening! It's terrible. Can't you make him stop? Can't you make him leave?" she sobbed.

Mr. Abe reached over and gently patted Carona's arm, "No, little one, we can't...but you can."

Nadie, who'd been hanging on to Mr. Abe's every word quickly inquired, "If we're part of the Legend, then we're the ones who are supposed to get rid of the General and save Boardland?"

"You're the only ones who can. The Legend started shortly after the General took over Boardland. No matter what we tried, we couldn't beat him and his Fingers. We felt so helpless. I guess to lessen the hopelessness we felt, someone started a story. It told of three children, each one having been students in Room 7, coming to Boardland to save us. The Legend foretold that only someone who was real, from the other side of the Blackboard, who couldn't be erased by the General, could be victorious. As time went by the story grew and even names, your names, were somehow attached to the story. It became our Legend of Hope, our promise of freedom."

"So as Flicker told us," expressed Caleb, "this is just the right time, I mean the right time for us to have come?"

"Very much so," Mr. Abe replied, "the very best of times."

"Why is this the very best time?" a curious Carona asked.

"Boardland is getting more and more crowded. Room 7 is creating drawings, words, and numbers faster than we can process and place them. Because of this, the General has decided to raise his artistic standards and cleanse Boardland of more undesirables. He plans to start by erasing all of Abstractshire and everyone and everything assigned to live there. He says that any drawing, word, or number that isn't completely legible or totally recognizable for what he thinks the artist intended it to be, should be smudged and erased as soon as it comes through the blackboard. Therefore, Abstractville has become obsolete," Mr. Abe explained.

"That's insane!" Caleb interjected. "Who does he think made him King? Can't the Great Illuminator do anything to stop him?"

"I understand your anger. You can only imagine how we feel," Mr. Abe continued. "All dictators soon come to believe that they are so important and powerful that they actually own that which they control by their brute power and greed. General Eraser has reached that point. He has lost all sense of reason, become totally selfish, and feels that he should destroy anyone who disagrees with him. In your world you refer to men like this as evil. The Great Illuminator does reign over the day by controlling the light in Boardland. He also has helpers in the form of Beams and Rays."

"You mean like Flicker and Gleam?" Carona asked.

"Exactly," Mr. Abe replied. "They do have certain powers. It is difficult for the General to stop them, but they in turn can't stop the General, only slow him down and make it more difficult for him and his Fingers to harm things."

"Then how can we help?" Nadie asked.

"Good question. The Legend doesn't tell us how the three Talbots will rid Boardland of this evil, only that you will find a way to do it," Mr. Abe replied.

"Wow!" Caleb exclaimed. "I haven't got a clue."

"I'm not concerned. The three of you will find a way, of that I'm sure," Mr. Abe concluded with a grin.

"Gleam and I and our other friends will help, if you need it," Flicker added.

"You know, Caleb," Carona noted, "the General can't erase us so he really can't hurt us, isn't that right Mr. Abe?"

"Good point, Carona," replied Mr. Abe. "But that doesn't mean he can't grab you, tie you up and put you all in prison. We may be mostly chalk, but in Boardland things do have substance."

"That's true, Carona," Flicker interjected. "Remember that black and white Border Collie you petted just as we came into Realtown?"

"The cute one that talked and got my hand all chalky?"

"Yes, but when you petted him, wasn't his body solid and firm?" Flicker continued.

"Ah, chalky but I sure felt him."

"There you go, Caleb," Mr. Abe noted. "You probably won't be destroyed, but that doesn't mean you can't be harmed or neutralized by the General."

"Then we're still not strong enough to defeat him," Caleb replied.

"That's not quite true," Flicker said. "According to the Legend and the Illuminator, you do have some special powers you can use."

"Like what powers?" Nadie asked quickly.

"We don't actually know," Flicker replied. "What we do know is that you're not from Boardland and you're not made of chalk, so things here will be much different for you than other citizens. The Illuminator feels that as you adjust to Boardland you will discover powers that will help you save us."

"Adjust to being here?" Nadie exclaimed. "You mean we can't leave when we want?"

"I understand your concern, Nadie," Mr. Abe replied. "You can leave, but once again, the time has to be right. Certain things have to come together for you to leave."

"Then when is the time right and what things have to come together?" Nadie questioned.

Mr. Abe, trying to calm Nadie down replied, "Just like your arrival and the timing for when you came, the timing for when you leave has not been shared with us. Our Legend doesn't say. But I can assure you that you will return home again, soon."

"Wow," Caleb sighed as he rubbed his brow. "This all is amazing. We're supposed to save Boardland, but we don't know how. Then we're supposed to be able to go home, but we don't know when or how. There is an awful lot to learn and figure out here. Are you sure the Legend refers to the three of us? Maybe it is mistaken and it meant someone else?"

Mr. Abe grinned and said, "No, Caleb, the more I see of the three of you the more I know the Legend was right. We'll all have to wait and see. I just hope that you will be able to figure things out before General Eraser does his evil deed."

"Thanks, Mr. Abe, no pressure here," Caleb replied. "I can't speak for Carona or Nadie, but I certainly don't know enough yet about Boardland to be able to figure out how we can defeat the General. I have read that in matters of conflicts and wars you need to know and understand your adversaries before you can find a way to defeat them. I guess our first job is to learn more about Boardland and more about the General and how he operates."

"Very good," Mr. Abe replied. "See, you've already developed a plan."

"That's probably the only thing we can do at this point," Nadie agreed.

"I sure hope we discover our powers soon," Carona shared. "I'm the smallest and I'll need all the powers I can get."

Suddenly they were all startled by a loud banging on the front door. Mr. Abe immediately stood up. Caleb could see that he was both surprised and concerned about the noise.

"It's way too late for a visitor. The only people moving around Boardland this late at night would be the General and his Fingers. Flicker, if you don't mind would you take the Talbots to the basement?"

Caleb looked over at Nadie who was already heading in the direction Flicker had taken Curly. Carona was right behind her.

"Of course," Flicker replied as he followed the girls.

"Do you think the General knows we've arrived in Boardland?" Caleb quietly asked.

"Only if one of his Fingers happened to see you watching the parade and realized from a distance that you were too real to be drawings. Of course, there is always the possibility that one of his spies saw you as you entered Realtown."

"He has spies in Realtown?" Caleb asked.

"Probably several. Don't all paranoid dictators? Unfortunately, even here some want to gain favors by turning on their own. Now you'd better hurry," Mr. Abe replied.

As Caleb raced to catch up with Flicker, Mr. Abe headed towards the door. He made sure Caleb was out of sight before he opened it. Standing on the front porch were three Fingers, including Sergeant Tall One. Mr. Abe smiled, and then tipped his hat.

"Good evening Sergeant, to what do I owe this honor?"

The Sergeant took a step forward and peered around Mr. Abe into the room. "Sorry to have bothered you so late. The General and I were merely passing by as he made his rounds cleansing the land. We'd heard that a stray Scribble may have entered Realtown, and you know we can't have that. Why think of how the residents would feel if that kind of riff raff were visiting."

Caleb had not followed Flicker and the others down into the basement. Instead he'd stopped just past the first door to listen and evaluate the situation.

"I certainly do understand your concern and I can assure you that I've not seen a Scribble running around outside," Mr. Abe replied.

"Humph," Sergeant Tall One replied. "Then have you seen any drawings new to Boardland arrive in Realtown today? We have evidence of some very real looking footprints on the chalky surface of the road leading into town."

Abe was perturbed he hadn't thought about the Talbots' footprints earlier but quickly regained his composure. "Oh, those would be from several of our residents who had gone to watch the parade and celebrate the General's birthday today. They just returned to town a short time ago."

"I see. That could be what we saw."

"Is there anything else I can help you with?" Mr. Abe politely asked.

As Sergeant Tall One took one more look into the house he replied, "No, not for now. The General sends his regards."

"And mine back to the General," Mr. Abe replied as he slowly closed the door.

Mr. Abe made his way to the closest front window carefully pulling a corner of the curtain back to make sure Sergeant Tall One and his soldiers had left.

"That was a close one!" Caleb exclaimed and Mr. Abe, startled, turned from the window. "I thought you were waiting in the basement?"

"I'm sorry, I just had to hear what the Fingers were saying just in case we needed to make a run for it."

"That I can understand," Mr. Abe replied.

"I guess we have to be more careful. I never thought of concealing our footprints. I keep forgetting that everything has a chalky surface."

"I should have known better myself," Mr. Abe continued.

At that moment Flicker and the girls appeared.

"Is everything okay?" Nadie asked.

Caleb turned and said, "For now it is, but we really have to be more careful with things like our footprints. This gets more complicated every moment."

Mr. Abe pulled up his coat sleeve and peered at a band around his wrist that looked like a large watch.

"It's getting late and I'm sure you're tired from your journey. There are two guest rooms upstairs you are welcome to use tonight, but we'd better find you another place to stay tomorrow. I have the feeling that my home will be watched now."

"Thanks," Nadie replied, "But what happens tomorrow?"

"We really need to explore Boardland if we're ever going to find a way to get rid of the General," noted Caleb.

"Yes, yes, you need to carefully sleuth around. You'd better go into the Forest of Memories first and find a place to stay," Flicker interjected.

"The Forest of Memories?" Carona repeated.

"It's really the best place for you to hide when you're not exploring. The General and his Fingers seldom enter it. They're afraid." Flicker replied.

"Perfect," Caleb shared. "We're supposed to hang out somewhere even the General doesn't want to go. Now why is that?"

"For all chalk drawings who have a conscience, the forest can create certain visions or phantom memories that can be either pleasing or very frightening. They may see their future or their past, if they even have one. It's a very disturbing place for drawings," Mr. Abe replied.

"Won't that happen to us?" Nadie asked.

"I'm not really sure," Mr. Abe answered. "We've never had real people for visitors. But I'm quite sure that it won't have the same effect on you since here again you're not chalk drawings! Now up to your rooms and I'll see you in the morning."

At the top of the stairs the Talbots found two nicely furnished rooms both having double beds. Nadie and Carona took the one on the left while Caleb took the other. Both rooms had views of the backyard.

Even in the dark, they could make out a yard that was mostly lawn along with two large elm trees and several beds of flowers, mostly roses and dahlias. A rope swing hung from the largest tree.

"Nadie, Nadie," Carona called out, "Can I swing tomorrow?"

Nadie, also looking out the window, replied, "Maybe we need to see what tomorrow brings."

"And what does tomorrow bring?" Caleb asked as he entered their room.

"I wish I knew," Nadie replied as she turned and saw Caleb behind them. "But right about now I wish we hadn't been in such a hurry to go through the blackboard."

"That's exactly what I was thinking," he answered.

"Looks like before we can leave we need to complete our mission, if the Legend about us is right, Caleb," said Nadie.

"Do we have a choice?" he replied. "Anyway, we need to be very careful and find out exactly what powers we have that can help us get rid of the General. Secondly, we need to discover a way out of Boardland so we can leave when we want. This 'time is right' thing I don't really understand. There's got to be a way back through the mountain you drew, Carona."

"I don't mind Boardland that much, but I always feel like I need to sneeze from all the chalk dust," Carona replied.

"Then we'd better shake out our blankets and get some sleep. We'll all need to be physically and mentally alert tomorrow," Nadie advised.

"What a glorious birthday it was, Captain. Not only did I provide a holiday, a parade, and a delicious cake for my subjects, I was able to erase many Scribbles, thanks to you and Sergeant Tall One."

"It is our pleasure to serve you, my General," the Captain replied.

"And how are the preparations coming for my, let's say, final plans?"

Captain Thumb bowed and replied, "Everything proceeds as you have commanded. The plan can be implemented within four days, on Monday!"

"Fine, that should certainly make more room in Boardland for those artistic works that are truly worthy."

"However, General, one of our spies believes that many of your subjects feel the Legend is true and already underway."

"The Legend is true and underway?" yelled the General. "You mean to tell me that somehow three real people have entered Boardland and are now plotting against me? Impossible!"

"What a glorious birthday it was."

"Yet General, the spy says he has seen them!"

"Who is this spy?"

Captain Thumb could see the General's black eyes growing larger as his breathing became quicker. He knew he had to be careful. "He is one of our most trusted spies and has access to many places. His intelligence has always been accurate. However, it is possible he could be wrong. I just want you to be aware of all the intelligence we gather. In your wisdom, you, as always, will use it as you see fit."

"Yes, I must think this all through, so we can show the people how wrong they are regarding the Legend. Send out more patrols to scour Boardland for anyone who speaks of this Legend or appears to be an outsider, if that's even possible! They will find my hospitality and dungeon most uninviting!"

"Your orders will be carried out immediately, my General," Captain Thumb replied, breathing a sigh of relief as he left quickly.

Chapter Four

Spring and the Map

In the morning as Caleb looked out the window he noticed that several clouds had appeared in the sky. In the distance he also thought he saw a large bird flying near them.

He knew he was as confused this morning as he'd been the day before. Boardland's tragic situation was none of their doing or really any of their business. Yet the Legend was so specific, and Flicker, Gleam, and Mr. Abe knowing their names really puzzled him.

Obviously in some way he and his sisters were a part of this strange land. As for the how and why he didn't have a clue. Suddenly his thoughts were interrupted by a knocking on his door.

Upon opening it, he saw Mary Todd smiling at him. It was a weird kind of smile, one that appears when the person smiling knows something you don't and doesn't intend to let you know what it is.

"Good morning. Would you like some breakfast before you go? Your sisters are already in the kitchen."

"Yes, sure," Caleb muttered back. "That would be fine."

As he followed her into the kitchen, he spotted Mr. Abe, Carona, and Nadie sitting at a large table. On the table was an assortment of fruit, breads, and candy which were barely identifiable. He took a seat next to Carona.

"I hope you were able to sleep some last night. I know how disconcerting it can be to be in such an unusual environment," Mr. Abe shared.

"Yes to both, Mr. Abe, and thank you for your hospitality and concern," Caleb replied as he rubbed Carona's head. "You two were up early this morning."

Nadie quickly replied. "Carona spotted the tree swing in the backyard yesterday and just had to try it before we left."

"And I was able to go higher than I've ever gone in a swing before, Caleb," Carona added gleefully, "although I did get a bit chalky".

"And sneezed a lot," Nadie added.

"I'm glad you enjoyed it," Caleb replied. "I don't see Curley. Did he leave?"

"Yes, he left early this morning to sneak back to his place in Abstractshire. By the way, you're welcome to anything you'd like on the table," Mr. Abe offered.

Caleb wasn't sure what to try although he was hungry since none of them had eaten since lunch the day before.

"I ate a banana and an apple," Carona shared. "Mrs. Abe got most of the chalk off them for me. They tasted almost real!"

"We're sorry our food isn't what you're used to," Mr. Abe stated. "We really don't grow much here. We have very little water, and if rain is ever drawn, it creates havoc in Boardland because of the chalk. Our food mostly consists of things drawn by children on the board. You will get used to the strange variety of edibles they have created. As for us, being drawings, most of us eat very little or nothing."

As Caleb reached for an apple and banana he suggested that Nadie and Carona take some in their backpacks for later since he didn't know when they'd find food again. Mr. Abe mentioned that wouldn't be necessary because Mary had packed food in a backpack for them along with some bottled water.

"We really appreciate your hospitality and food, Mary," Caleb said as she nodded. "We do need to be going."

As Mr. Abe stood up he spoke. "You three have quite a task ahead of you. I'm always here if you need anything. Flicker and some other friends will help you find a place to hide in the Forest of Memories."

Flicker met them on the front porch. "We really need to hurry. The General lives at the other end of Realtown and often comes this way in the morning."

"Let's go then," Caleb replied as he moved forward, anxious to get to safety. "How far is the Forest of Memories?"

Flicker, who had changed from a fast walk to a jog, answered, "A little over three miles, but we'll need to stay off the roads, since the General may know of your arrival and have his Fingers out looking for you." Flicker didn't want to startle the Talbots as he noticed two Fingers on horses approaching from down the street.

Caleb looked around at Nadie and Carona and noted that like him, neither of them appeared to be getting winded. "We could move faster if necessary," he mentioned to Flicker who replied, "Great idea!" as he increased his speed. Caleb, realizing that since Flicker was a light beam and could probably move as fast as he wanted, decided to pick up the pace even more. Soon they'd covered over two miles dodging trees and shrubs while no one seemed to be tiring. So, Caleb decided to run even faster to see what would happen. As he did the rest of the group simply kept up with him. He noted that they were now probably running faster than most animals he'd ever seen. Even a mountain lion would have trouble catching them. He found himself smiling and thoroughly enjoying the speed so he jumped forward in his excitement. To his surprise he actually stayed in the air for about fifty feet before lightly setting back down.

When the group approached a hilly area comprised mostly of large fir and pines, Flicker began to slow down to a brisk walk. Caleb saw him look around and smile.

"I believe you just discovered one of the special skills you have in Boardland," Flicker noted as they approached the edge of the forest.

Carona, who had been giggling the last few blocks, gleefully exclaimed, "Let me guess, running faster than an antelope!"

With that Nadie added, "That was exhilarating. I never would have believed it!"

"And jumping," Caleb added as he bent down and jumped twenty feet into the air.

"I have to admit," Flicker offered, "being a beam with almost unlimited speed allows me to escape from the General whenever I feel threatened. It seems the three of you may have that ability too. That should make it extremely difficult for his Fingers to capture you if you're vigilant."

"And I have to say I had my doubts about the Legend and our special abilities in Boardland," Caleb replied. "But after this I can't wait to see what other skills emerge."

Flicker looked over his shoulder and suggested they move on into the Forest of Memories for in the distance he spied the two riders approaching.

The forest was dense and quiet. The trees towered above them blotting out most of the Illuminator's rays. The shadows seemed to be constantly moving, creating an eerie environment. Flicker moved slowly and cautiously as Caleb noticed him occasionally glance back.

Finally, Carona broke the silence, "Flicker, are we going to pass through any meadows? I'd really like to find some more wildflowers like the ones I drew in my mountain picture."

"There are a few smaller meadows in the forest and I believe some even have flowers," Flicker replied as he moved forward.

"And I'm just glad I'm somewhere Mother can't yell at me," Nadie quipped. "Even here it's hard to forget how selfish she can be."

"Darn," Caleb said as he looked up through the shadows to try to catch a glimpse of the Illuminator. "Rich and I still have a science project to finish for Mr. Sears' class when I get back."

Flicker turned and stopped. "I'm afraid you all will need to be more focused on your plan. From what I'm hearing, the Forest of Memories does have some effect on each of you. You can't let it distract you or fill your minds with unnecessary thoughts or memories."

"Wow," Nadie exclaimed. "It's kind of like day dreaming without knowing you're day dreaming!"

"You're fortunate not to be having memories that are so bad that they haunt and grab hold of you, filling your mind with pain. That's what usually happens to drawings that enter the forest. They seem to always have nightmarish thoughts of their abrupt creation and the knowledge that they're just chalk drawings!" Flicker explained.

As they hiked deeper into the forest, Nadie felt they were being watched if not followed. She moved closer to Caleb and whispered, "Do you feel like something is watching us?"

"Now that you mention it, I do. Several times I thought I saw something bounding behind a tree, but when I blinked it disappeared."

"I sure hope we weren't followed by the Fingers. Maybe it's just these weird shadows." She stopped and carefully scrutinized the forest around them.

Flicker paused, and then turned around. "I'm sorry, but I couldn't help but hear what you were saying." Both Nadie and Caleb looked at each other and wondered just how much Flicker could hear. "My hearing is quite pronounced, one of my gifts from the Illuminator. As to whether we were being followed the answer is yes. Two Fingers on horseback followed us as we left Realtown. That's why I'm glad we sped up. I didn't want to worry you so I kept an eye on them. They, as usual, stopped following us after we entered the Forest of Memories. However, once we came into the Forest a little Scribble has been watching us from a distance. I'm afraid she's not sure about the three of you and doesn't know quite what to do. If you don't mind I'll try to assure her you are friendly."

"Why would she be afraid? Doesn't she know the Legend?" Carona asked.

"Yes, but being a Scribble and one that the Fingers have orders to smudge, makes her extremely cautious. That's why she is hiding in the forest even with the prospect of having terrifying memories. Often one awful choice for someone is less harmful than making another. Each day many drawings in Boardland have to make that decision."

"You keep calling the Scribble 'she'", Nadie mentioned.

"She's a cute little Scribble, but she looks like a spring, without legs, so she has to bounce everywhere."

"What's her name?" Carona asked.

"Well, Spring of course. No one really knows what the artist had intended to draw. That was the best we could do," Flicker replied as he called out her name and let her know they were the Talbots from the Legend and were here to help her.

Immediately, after Flicker called, a Scribble, looking much like a spring, bounced towards them.

She was wearing a light green dress and had arms along with a girlish face bordered by blond hair.

"Are you sure it's all right, Flicker?" a high pitched young voice asked.

Flicker smiled and replied, "Yes, Spring, these are the Talbots and they've finally come."

Immediately Spring began to bounce and sing, "Finally we'll be free. The Eraser is going to flee. The Fingers will follow. We'll be merry tomorrow, and we'll all live happily!"

Carona immediately began to sing along with Spring as she continued singing and bouncing through another chorus of the same song. Caleb and Nadie couldn't help but laugh, but their laughter soon subsided as rising chalk dust filled the air.

"Spring, please, the dust is bothering the Talbots. Remember, they're not used to it," Flicker explained.

Instantly Spring stopped. "Oh, I'm sorry. I'm Spring, and you are Caleb, Nadie and Carona. I know all about you. You couldn't have come at a better time. I've been waiting so long. Why I was almost smudged by Captain Thumb just a week ago in Abstractshire. He thinks I'm too weird to be of value. But I know that I'm special and my creator knew exactly what he was doing when he..."

Flicker loudly cleared his throat. "Now Spring, we're glad you're all right but we really have to be finding a safe place in the forest for the Talbots to stay while they're developing their plan."

"Oh, oh, of course," she replied. "And I know a perfect place. It just arrived last night. I'll be happy to show you."

"That would be very kind of you," Caleb replied.

Spring turned while batting her eyes at Caleb. "You spoke to me! Caleb spoke to me, Flicker. See, even he knows I'm somebody special."

"Of course you are," Nadie interjected, "and we're going to find a way so you can live in Boardland forever...I hope."

"You're so nice too. Hurry, I'll show you," Spring replied as she bounded adroitly off in the same direction she'd just bounced in from.

Caleb rubbed his brow as they followed. He still couldn't believe they were in a place like Boardland talking to chalk characters who they were supposed to save from a fanatic eraser. He couldn't believe that every place they'd ever gone, both here and home, seemed to have its own problems.

Within minutes they were through the densest part of the forest and were entering one of those meadow clearings that Flicker had told Carona about. There in the center was a large two storied pillared house with shuttered windows and white lace curtains.

Nadie let out a soft cry, like she was catching her breath. "Caleb, Carona, that's my house!" she exclaimed. "That's the one I drew on the blackboard before we passed through!"

"I can't believe it!" Caleb replied. "I'm sure it is because right next to it is the willow tree I drew, but I don't see my eagles."

"Now that's a real coincidence. For the life of me I can't figure out why some drawings turn up where they do. No offense, Nadie, but that house will probably end up in Primitivepality. But as long as it's here, it should be a safe place for you to stay."

"See, I knew it would be the perfect place," Spring added.

Flicker reached into his white robe and pulled out a rolled-up piece of paper. "Mr. Abe gave this to me for you," he said as he handed the paper to Caleb. "It's a detailed map of Boardland, at least as detailed as possible with things changing as often as they do. You'll all need to study it if you expect to move around without being seen by the Fingers."

"Be sure to thank him for us, Flicker. We'll look it over when we get inside before we start exploring," Caleb replied.

"Then I'll be on my way for now. The Illuminator has some other tasks for me. Oh, by the way, since this is your first full day in Boardland you'll need to know about Recess."

"Recess?" inquired Nadie.

"That's because Boardland is created by Room 7. Room 7 has recess at ten-thirty each week day. Everyone leaves the room while the Creator turns the lights out and nothing happens on the blackboard. In

Boardland, everything stops for half an hour and all the drawings can't move. Most take a quick nap. Only beams and rays from the Illuminator can still get around. Since you're not drawings, I'm sure it won't affect you, just one more little detail. Anyway, I'll get back soon."

Carona, looking concerned, asked, "But aren't you going to show us around and look out for us?"

"I'll be back, Carona, but you three have as much ability to move around Boardland as safely as I do, at least if you're careful. Until then, Spring will be more than happy to answer any questions you have. She's really quite adept at surviving in Boardland," Flicker replied as he sped off.

"I'll be glad to help you and I won't be any trouble at all. I'll just wait out here and when you're ready for me just call. I can't believe that I'm getting to help the famous Talbots!" Spring exclaimed as she bounced towards the nearest group of trees.

The furnishings inside of Nadie's house were very basic, but there were beds, weird beds, but beds, and a cooler with cool, but chalky food. Nadie couldn't figure out how a house she'd just drawn would have such furnishings on the inside.

She pondered this while they all sat down at the kitchen table and Caleb opened the map.

"This is an amazing map," Carona observed as they all peered at it.

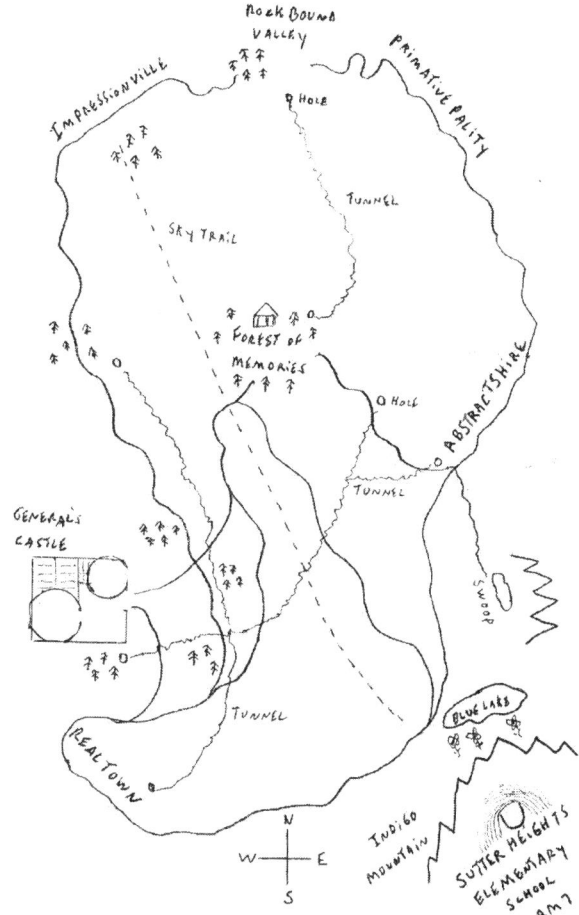

"They all sat down at the kitchen table and opened the map."

"I've never seen a map like this before. It has all the basic features such as the four towns, roads, a few lakes, rivers and mountain ranges, but it also has a lot of unusual stuff. There seem to be tunnels all over the place, even under the towns, and I guess all these lines are paths or trails?" Caleb asked.

"I'm sure they must be," Nadie agreed, "But what are these marks in the sky?"

"They look like the flight routes on a map I saw in a magazine on the plane when we flew to New York to see Father a few years ago. You know, the places the plane could go."

"Yeah, but why?" Carona asked. "I haven't seen anything in the sky since we've been here except the Illuminator, some clouds, and of course Gleam."

"I don't know about those lines, but these trails are probably the safest way around. If the Fingers move on trucks and horses then staying in the trees or brush on out of the way trails would probably be wise. If they happen to come along we can quickly hide. As for the tunnels, maybe they have something to do with that thing I saw in the mountain. I believe Flicker called it a "Tunneler'. Maybe they dug all these. The map does show their entrances," Caleb noted.

"If that's what they actually are," Nadie expressed as she pointed towards a large strange marking near Realtown. "What do you suppose this is?"

"It could be a large building," Nadie replied.

"It looks like a walled castle to me," Carona interjected.

"I suppose it could be where the General and his Fingers hang out. Flicker did say he lived near Realtown," Caleb explained. "That's the place we should scope out. We need to know as much as we can about the General and how many soldiers he has. But on our way, I suggest we take a peek at the other three towns before we double back to Realtown and the General's."

"I think we should leave right now," suggested Carona. "I can't wait to run again."

"We may be super-fast and jump high but we still need to be careful," cautioned Caleb, "even though we have two special powers."

Nadie and Carona looked at each other and shrugged their shoulders not knowing what Caleb was talking about. Finally, Nadie asked, "Okay, what are they?"

Caleb smiled and said, "First our ability to jump high and move fast..."

"And the second?" Carona quickly asked.

"Recess!" Caleb exclaimed.

Carona looked at him still not comprehending, "We don't need a recess for naps."

"Right," Caleb replied. "But everyone else does. Those thirty minutes let us move around without being seen. We could even check out the General's place while he and his Fingers are still and napping. They won't even know we've been there!"

"Maybe we can pull this off and find a way to get rid of the General," quipped Nadie.

Caleb pointed to the map.

"Then let's follow this trail that leads through the forest and along these hills to Abstractshire and Primitivepality. Then we can go to Impressionville, and end up near Realtown at the General's around..."

"I know," Carona shouted, "at ten thirty!"

"Good plan," Nadie added. "That way we'll get a quick look at the main parts of Boardland and gather useful information."

Chapter Five

The Tunnelers and the General

By now the Talbots were feeling hopeful and excited. For the first time they felt they had a chance to develop a plan that would allow them to save Boardland. Caleb knew they still had a lot to learn. Every little piece of information could make the difference between success and failure. However, sometimes the more that is known about something, the more questions need to be asked. Some of the other strange markings and structures placed on the map Mr. Abe had sent them still worried him.

Out front, Spring was waiting. Caleb showed her the map and the trail they planned to take to explore Boardland. She agreed that going the way he'd selected would be the safest, and then bounded toward the trail. Even though they could outrun her, Spring still moved rapidly so they stayed just behind her. Caleb could see the excitement in Carona's and Nadie's eyes when they moved like the wind through the trees and brush. As they turned a corner, Caleb saw Spring suddenly disappear and heard a high-pitched voice yell, "I forgot!" He immediately stopped running and Carona and Nadie almost knocked him down.

"Hey, why did you stop so fast?" Nadie exclaimed.

Caleb, who was looking down, simply pointed. There in front of them was a deep hole in the middle of the trail. At the bottom they could make out Spring.

"Are you all right, Spring?" Caleb yelled.

For a moment there was silence, but finally they heard Spring. "I'm all right, just a little embarrassed that I didn't know a Tunneler's hole was here."

Caleb pulled the map from his pocket.

"That's strange, it's not listed on my map."

"Things change fast in Boardland," Spring replied. "I may need your help in getting out. I don't think I can bounce that high."

"We haven't got a rope and there are no long sticks or branches around," Nadie replied.

"I know I can jump high enough," Caleb noted. "I'll drop down into the hole with you. Then you can hold onto me as I jump us both back out. You can't weigh that much."

"Okay, but be careful," Spring replied.

Caleb carefully dropped about fifteen feet down into the tunnel hole. As he landed, Spring seemed to have disappeared. Caleb saw tunnels to the right and left but no Spring. Then he heard Spring's high-pitched voice coming from down the tunnel to his left.

"Help, I'm here with the Talbots. They're going to help all of us. Where are you taking me?"

"Someone's grabbed Spring. Quick, drop down in with me so we can find her. We need to keep together," Caleb yelled up.

Immediately Carona and Nadie dropped into the tunnel. Caleb was already heading in the direction of Spring's voice. The low tunnel caused Caleb and Nadie to bend down as they moved yet it was high enough for Carona. Even though it was below ground it was dusty and dry with the chalk filled earth giving off a slight purple glow. It caused just enough light to allow them to see. Despite the low tunnel, they all managed to move like the wind. As they rounded a turn, they entered a larger cavern where they could stand up as they ran. Now Caleb could see Spring being dragged along by several Tunnelers. Their brown furry bodies and human like faces with large front teeth were clearly visible.

"I see Spring and the Tunnelers just in front of us. We should be able to catch up with them any minute!" Caleb yelled.

The Tunnelers seemed surprised that they were being out run by their pursuers so they decided to turn and make a stand. The Talbots kept running until they were right next to them.

"Leave us! Get out of our tunnel!" the gravelly deep voice of the largest and hairiest Tunneler yelled as all menacingly bared their large front teeth.

Nadie yelled back, "You have our friend. Let her go!"

Another Tunneler yelled back, "This is our home! None of you belong here! Now leave!"

Caleb stood as straight as he could and stepped close to the hairiest one who needed to look straight up to see him.

"We are not drawings! We're not here to hurt you. We've come to Boardland to help rid you of General Eraser. Don't you know about the Legend? We are the Talbots!"

Caleb waited for a moment, not sure what he should do next. He did turn enough to see that down the tunnel behind him several more Tunnelers had gathered and were blocking their way out. Carona gasped as she too noticed their presence.

The largest Tunneler stared at Caleb for a moment then quickly thrust out his claw like hand and slapped Caleb hard on his leg. Caleb knew he shouldn't move or look surprised even though the drawing had probably left a bruise. So, he stood his ground and stared back. Slowly his antagonist let his hold on Spring slip away. Caleb felt himself relax a little.

Suddenly the largest Tunneler yelled, "No chalk dust!" Caleb wasn't sure what that meant, although it didn't sound like a further challenge. "He's not a drawing!" came another cry.

At that point all the Tunnelers slowly began to close in on the four of them with outreached claws. "Just stand still," Caleb whispered softly as each one of them was lightly rubbed by one Tunneler after another.

The largest Tunneler ceased baring his teeth even though they still stuck out. "Then you're not here to harm or erase us?" his husky voice asked.

"No, of course not! We came here to help. Mr. Abe knows we're the three Talbots which the Legend foretold. We're exploring Boardland to come up with a plan to help you get rid of the General," Caleb replied.

"Then welcome. We usually don't like visitors to our underground world. Matter of fact, we stay to ourselves and are seldom bothered by the General and his Fingers. Oh, I guess I should be more polite. My name is Groff. I'm the leader of the Tunnelers, as those above call us. I believe your names would be Caleb, Nadie, and Carona Talbot."

"Everyone knows our names!" Carona again expressed.

"Of course we know the Legend, although we never thought much about it since we live peaceably underground," Groff replied.

Nadie seemed a bit confused. "Why aren't you bothered by the General? Haven't any of you ever been erased?"

Groff looked saddened.

"Of course, we have lost a few friends, but that's only when one of us has broken our laws and spent too much time on the surface or gone some place we shouldn't have. The General's afraid of us ever since we trapped several of the Fingers he sent to smudge us in one of our tunnels. We tricked them and collapsed the tunnel on top of them. After that he's not bothered us unless he sees us on the surface. So we live our lives the way we want."

Caleb wasn't sure what to say. Carona immediately spoke up. "Don't you want to be free to be on the surface whenever you want? Wouldn't you like to see the General and his Fingers gone from Boardland?"

"Of course we would, but at what cost? There aren't many of us left. The artist who drew us years ago has never returned and others don't bother to create drawings that have to do with things beneath the earth. So, we exist as we are."

Groff's statements made Carona sad. Caleb and Nadie also seemed to empathize with the Tunnelers' plight and understand why they tried to keep out of the problems faced by drawings above. Caleb also realized that if he could gain their support for their plans to rid Boardland of the General, the Tunnelers, with their tunnels all around, could give them a great advantage.

"What if we could get rid of the General? Would you at least let us use your tunnels when necessary to move without being noticed?" he asked.

Groff stared at Caleb for a moment then pointed at two other Tunnelers and motioned for them to come forward. The three of them moved a few feet down the Tunnel. The Talbots could hear their quiet yet gravelly voices mumbling away as they seemed to be discussing Caleb's request. After a few moments Groff stepped forward.

"We have never allowed what you request. Intruders, like we thought the Scribble was, have always been dealt with harshly. Yet we know the Legend. We would like to see the General erased from Boardland. Since we wouldn't have to expose ourselves to the surface and since using our tunnels could help you rid us of this menace, the Council has decided to give you our permission."

"Then we thank you for your assistance. We will use your tunnels only when we have to. But I have one more favor to ask," Caleb said as he unrolled Mr. Abe's map.

Groff and the others looked at it curiously. Groff traced his fingers over several of the lines. Caleb could see that they were quite interested in many of the topographical features. The Tunnelers seemed alert and intelligent. This was the first time Caleb and his sisters actually had a chance to observe them. Beyond their furry bodies, claw like hands, and their pronounced front teeth, their faces seemed surprisingly human. They looked like a group of men examining a map. Caleb still couldn't understand how or why all the drawings came to life as living, intelligent beings.

"Very interesting," Groff finally remarked. "I'd be curious to know how the drawing who made this map learned of so many of our tunnels?"

"Actually, it was given to us by Mr. Abe," Caleb replied.

Groff actually smiled, "Of course. Only he and the Illuminator would know our secrets."

"What I need to know from you is whether or not the map is correct...in regards to your tunnels?"

"Most of them are marked on it. Some are not. But in case this map gets into the wrong hands and discloses our tunnel system we will keep the knowledge of those tunnels to ourselves. I'm sure you understand," Groff replied.

"We can respect that. One of those unmarked tunnels was apparently the one that Spring, the Scribble, fell into," Caleb noted.

"Yes," Groff replied. "Now we have a favor to ask of the three of you."

"Anything we can do to help," Caleb said.

"We don't want you showing this map to anyone else except your most trusted friends. Also, whenever you use our tunnels, you keep us informed as to your plans to rid us of that wretched General."

Caleb turned to Nadie and Carona and they both nodded yes. "We agree," Caleb replied. "Now we need to hurry. We were planning on visiting Abstractshire and the other towns on our way to the General's home. We hoped to be there by Recess so we could poke around unnoticed during their naps."

"Then I suggest you follow this tunnel which comes up near the General's place, since Recess quickly approaches, and visit the other towns later," Groff replied as he pointed at the map while Caleb folded it up. "As for us, we don't recognize Recess since we remain virtually in the dark all the time."

"I am curious about the purple glow in the tunnels. In the larger caverns it is even brighter and allows us to see."

"Your eyes must be as sensitive as ours in the tunnels," he said as he grinned. "The drawings above ground don't have that ability and there's another reason why they leave us alone."

"That may be another ability we have," Nadie noted.

"We hope you have many more for we consider you our friends," Groff replied. "But now you must go if you expect to examine the General's place during Recess. Satch here, one of my most trusted friends, will lead the way. I know you'll do more than keep up with him."

"Thank you, Groff," Caleb replied.

Carona added, "And we consider you our friends too."

Instantly Satch took off down the tunnel. The three of them took a moment to catch up. Satch was certainly one of the fastest and possibly the slenderest Tunneler. He rounded turns and sprinted the straight ways as though he had each step memorized. Other tunnel entrances and systems came and went as Satch moved like a predator on a hunt.

Caleb still wasn't exactly sure what they'd be looking for when they got to the General's, but he realized that as they moved around Boardland they gained useful information that could help them develop a plan. Nadie was right on his heels and Carona, with her cheerful nature, grinned as she seemed to enjoy every moment of their tunnel run. Spring, who as a Scribble realized her precarious position with the Tunnelers, had remained very quiet while she bounded along behind Carona.

Finally, Satch began to slow as they approached an arm of the tunnel that turned up. He looked back at the four of them and pointed as he grinned, turned, and immediately retraced his steps back down the tunnel.

"Wow! I guess he must have an important date," Caleb shared as they watched Satch's furry body disappear.

"He did point up, didn't he?" Nadie asked.

"I'm sure this must be the tunnel opening near the General's place," Carona replied. "I don't believe that Groff would lie to us."

"Since I can't be of any help to you during Recess, I better go back to the Forest of Memories where I will be safe," Spring exclaimed. "But I'll be near if you need me."

"We really appreciate your help, Spring, and we understand," Nadie replied. "We'll see you back at the house."

Celeb knew that Spring was vulnerable. Either way, the Tunnelers didn't like Scribbles in their tunnels and the General would quickly erase her if she were caught. She was wise to leave.

While Spring bounded down the tunnel they cautiously moved up. "I'm not sure what to expect in Boardland anymore," Caleb said. "But I agree with you, Carona, that Groff wasn't lying to us, so let's take a peek."

As they surfaced, they pushed up what seemed like long blades of grass that lay over and hung into the opening, virtually concealing it. When they crawled out, they found themselves surrounded by bushes which of course were covered with chalk dust.

"Try not to sneeze," Caleb whispered. "We don't know how close we are and certainly don't want to give ourselves away before Recess," he added. As he looked at his watch he noted it was ten-twenty-five.

"Caleb, look to your right," Nadie whispered. "We're at the base of a large wall or something."

"I see it," Caleb replied.

"It looks like we came up right outside the walled grounds of someone's home, hopefully the General's," said Carona.

"These Tunnelers really know where to dig," Nadie replied.

"We need to take a look on the other side," Caleb said as he moved towards the wall and looked up. "I'd say it's about sixteen feet high. I know we can jump it. I'll go over first. If it's the General's I'll toss this stone back over and you can follow."

"And if it's not?" Nadie asked.

"Then I'll be right back, but give me a minute to look around," Caleb said as he bent down, jumped, and easily cleared the wall.

Caleb was surprised by the small cloud of yellow dust he stirred up when he landed in the middle of a large bush. He laid there for a moment, trying not to sneeze. He spotted a large stone building with a high conical tower about two hundred feet away through more trees and bushes. When he crawled closer he could see two figures standing against the side of what appeared to be a castle. This is the General's he thought when he realized that the figures were actually two Fingers. He watched them for a moment before crawling back to the wall and tossing the stone over. He made sure he was clear of the yellow bush.

Sure enough, Carona soon dropped over. Caleb pulled her away from the bush and quietly whispered "shh" while telling her not to sneeze. A moment later Nadie landed. She also caused a small yellow cloud that rapidly dissipated.

Caleb pointed toward the castle, signaling them to follow as he crawled to a large tree twenty feet away.

"There are two Fingers against the castle so it must be the General's," he whispered. Both girls peered around the tree and nodded. Caleb looked at his watch and observed it was ten-twenty-nine. A moment later the Illuminator's light went out.

"What is that all about?" noted Nadie.

Carona whispered, "Our teacher always turns out the light in the room when we go out to recess and she goes to the office."

"Darn, hadn't thought of that. At least there is still a bluish glow. Look! Now I can make out the two Fingers who are sitting down against the side of the castle," Caleb replied. "Good thing we can see even when it's almost completely dark."

"I bet they're napping," Nadie added.

"We don't have time to wait. I'll get closer and signal you if they are," Caleb said as he crouched down and began to run from tree to tree approaching the two Fingers. Sure enough, they were sound asleep so he signaled his sisters. They made their way around to the front, finding two very large doors with two more Fingers asleep next to them. Caleb grabbed a wheel shaped door opener using both hands and slowly turned it. The right door opened. They peered in and entered.

"Wow," Nadie whispered as they stepped into a massive room with the ceiling at least four stories above them. There was also a light afterglow inside which allowed them to see. "This is like the movies we've seen when someone visits the king. It has all the trappings of a castle receiving room," she whispered. "Look, there is even a throne raised up at the other end with a large picture of the General hanging above it!'

"Looks like the General made himself King," Caleb whispered back. "I wonder where everyone is?"

"Probably in their beds taking naps if they're like us," Carona replied as she moved towards the throne.

"I see spears and swords mounted along the walls but no modern weapons like guns and things," Nadie noted.

"Fourth graders don't draw guns on the blackboard and I don't see why a teacher would either," Carona mentioned.

"Good point, Carona. There probably aren't any in Boardland. That's one more important thing to note," Caleb replied.

As they walked down the hall they entered another large room dominated by a massive table. They stopped momentarily when they noticed four

Fingers sitting at the long table with their heads down. "Must be the dining area," Nadie whispered.

"Over here is a wide spiral staircase going up and down" Carona mentioned as she started to walk up.

"Wait!" Nadie cautioned. "The General's probably up there."

Caleb immediately started up the stairs, "Then that's where we have to go. You have to know your enemy. Besides he's got to be napping too."

As the stairs twisted up, hallways and doors appeared. Nadie turned to go down the first hallway. "We can't try all the doors in such a short time. We only have another twenty minutes," Caleb reminded them. "Besides, these lower rooms are more than likely for his guards and guests. I say we try the highest floor just below the tower. Dictators are usually paranoid, expecting the worst since they've made so many enemies. His room has got to be the hardest to get to."

Sure enough, as they rounded the last set of stairs leading to the top floor, they spotted two more Fingers resting against the wall. Behind them was a door larger than the others they'd passed.

"All I can say is that these things are sure weird looking," Nadie whispered as they stepped over the legs of the tallest Finger.

"You mean the funny faces on what must be their fingernails or the thin legs and arms coming out of the jointed finger?" Caleb whispered back.

"I think the artist was rather clever," Carona replied. She bent down to get a closer look at their faces. "They even have wrinkles on their knuckles...and look these have black and red uniforms and I saw some wearing brown."

As Nadie reached for the door knob, she paused. "Do you think it's locked from the inside?"

"I bet it's not with all the guards he has around. Besides he knows the other drawings have to nap for Recess at the same time," Caleb whispered.

Immediately Nadie opened the door. Again, the room was large and rounded like the outside tower. Curtains with pictures of various scenes drawn on them hung around the room. Predominantly featured in each picture was General Eraser looking wise and powerful. Across the room between two turret-like windows was a massive four poster bed with a black canopy. In the middle lay the General. Carona let out a short gasp as Nadie quickly placed her hand over Carona's mouth. The General was massive, at least eight feet tall. Most of his body looked just like the grayish black eraser Mrs. Durham used in Room 7. His squared face was surrounded by long black hair with a handle bar mustache. On a tall chair next to the bed hung his uniform, black with diagonal red stripes and an opposing white diagonal sash with silver stars.

"I can see why the rest of Boardland is afraid of this guy. Not only does he have delusions of grandeur but he's also a formidable looking man...or eraser, that is. An eraser that size can do a lot of damage," Caleb whispered.

Carona move closer to his bed. "Look, he has his arm over something. It looks like he's napping with a teddy bear or some kind of stuffed animal."

As Nadie approached "You're right, but it's not a teddy bear but a stuffed likeness of him! It's even wearing a uniform like the one on the chair! He's got himself for a teddy bear doll companion. This guy is really narcissistic!"

Caleb moved closer and carefully lifted the General's arm off the Little General doll, then grabbed it. "Quick, let's get out of here," he whispered as he hurried towards the door. His two surprised sisters followed Caleb as he sped down the stairs. At the bottom he paused and looked at his watch. "We have seven more minutes. Let's check downstairs before we go." Nadie and Carona nodded before they headed down.

The castle basement was well below ground. The afterglow lighting was even dimmer than above. Immediately they came to a room filled with small cells and three more sleeping Fingers. Along the walls the barred cells looked like ones seen in the jails of old western movies. Inside of them were many drawings. One was filled with numbers or letters with arms and legs that looked like R, S, and T, obviously Scribbles. They too were napping. Against one wall were arm and leg chains and many smaller erasers. Apparently, the General had grabbed any drawings of erasers that the students in Room 7 had ever drawn as soon as they appeared in Boardland. Only he and his Fingers were allowed to use that weapon.

"This must be where the General erases the drawings he doesn't like," Carona gasped, "at least the ones he didn't smudge already. This is awful! Let's let them out!"

Caleb smiled at Nadie and said, "Let's do it."

Caleb knew that when the General found his favorite sleep aid gone, he would be extremely agitated, and try to find out what happened to it. With the barred cells opened and the Scribbles running about, he'd know for sure it wasn't just a prank by a vengeful guard or drawing since they also would have been napping. The Talbots would be giving themselves away. But Caleb also figured that causing a little chaos and letting the General know what powers they had, might be a discomforting and grand calling card.

"Great idea!" he said as he took some keys off the nearest Finger. He unlocked then opened the barred doors. "Hopefully the Scribbles wake up first and run for it," he said. "And now we need to run for it," he added as they bounded up the stairs, through the great room and out towards the wall.

As soon as they reached the yellow bush, Nadie looked back. "The Fingers are moving. We just made it, but we better get over the wall before the General wakes!"

"Carona, quick, you jump first," Caleb exclaimed. Carona instantly jumped. "You next, Nadie," Caleb said as he looked over his shoulder and saw ten or more Fingers and several Scribbles running in all directions as the Illuminator's light was again at work. "On second thought let's jump together!" he exclaimed as they both jumped over. Once on the other side they found the bushes where the tunnel came up, pushed the grasses aside, and disappeared into the opening just as they heard horses thundering by above them.

"We need to be more careful. That was too close!" said Nadie.

Carona agreed, "Yes, but I'm glad we were able to free those Scribbles. I hope some managed to get away. That dungeon was awful."

"I do too," Nadie replied. "By the way, Caleb, why did you take the General's stuffed doll?"

"Impulse," he replied. "I saw that arrogant, narcissistic, evil drawing lying there and wanted to do something that would make him feel a little like he made others feel, so I grabbed it. I also knew it could come in handy as we develop our plan. I'd be willing to bet that big eraser would do anything to get his Little General back," Caleb continued as he zipped it into his school backpack.

"Where are we going now?" Carona asked.

"We need to take a look at Abstractshire since that's the town the General plans to erase," Nadie suggested.

"You're right," Caleb agreed. "We could use some help and I'll bet the Scribbles that are forced to live there would do anything to help us," he added as he opened the map. "It's not safe above so we better use the tunnels and find the closest opening to Abstractshire."

"I found one!" Carona said as she moved her finger across a tunnel opening that came up near Abstractshire.

"Then we'd better get moving," Nadie said glancing at the map and starting to run.

"Captain Thumb! Captain Thumb," yelled General Eraser.

The door to the General's room slowly opened as one of his guards peeked in sheepishly.

"My General, Captain Thumb is probably napping in his quarters, should I get him?"

"Of course, why else would I be calling for him you fool! Someone has been in my room!" the General, obviously upset, yelled out.

"But General, we have been guarding your door, even during Recess!"

"But you were asleep during Recess!" the General yelled again.

"Yes, my General. Everyone sleeps during Recess."

"Not everyone, you ignoramus. Someone wasn't sleeping and he stole something from my room! Now alert all my troops to comb the palace grounds and search in all directions. Arrest any drawing that is nearby...actually anything that can move that's nearby! ...and get me the Captain!"

Just then another face peered around the half-opened door. "Were, uhh, you asking for me, my General?" Captain Thumb cautiously asked.

"Who else? You are my Captain, aren't you? Or are you having memory problems again?"

"General you know that I..."

"Didn't you hear my orders? Send all my troops out to search in every direction and arrest anything near that can move. Then bring them to me!"

"Soldier, alert the men, immediately!" Captain Thumb yelled at the confused guard.

"Yes, my Captain!" the guard cried out as he grabbed the other guard who'd been hiding just around the corner and ran down the stairs.

"How could this be? You were in your own room with guards in front of your door. How could anyone come in and take something, especially during Recess?" the Captain asked.

The General's cheeks grew red. His black eyes began to bulge.

"Because the Legend is probably true you idiot! Only a real person could avoid napping during Recess. Only a real person would dare sneak into my palace, much less my room. Only a person who thought he could challenge my authority would dare steal my..."

"What did they steal, my General?" the Captain asked.

The General was obviously looking for the right words as he blubbered and momentarily mumbled. "The thing that was stolen, yes, it was a small, uh, doll likeness of myself, uhh, which I planned to give as an award to the first soldier who smudged the most Scribbles during our attack on Abstractshire. Yes, that's it, an award is what they took, and I want it back. The soldier I may give it to will be so disappointed."

"So, if that's the case, General, I need to alert the troops to be looking for real people, not drawings. Is that not true?"

"Exactly, and this is even more important. The men must be ordered to say nothing about the possibility of the Legend having begun or that the so-called Talbots from this Legend are actually in Boardland. You understand?"

"They will all be most careful or I personally will smudge the soldier who spreads such, uhh, rumors."

The General moved across the room towards the Captain who swallowed hard as the General's massive body blocked out the light, leaving the Captain in his shadow. He stopped, bent over and whispered in the Captain's ear. "These pretenders must be caught and disposed of immediately. Use every soldier we have. Interrogate everyone who's ever spied for us. We must know where they are and what they are up to. Do you understand?" he snarled.

"Clearly, my General!"

Chapter Six

Swoop and Special Powers

Again, Caleb and Nadie were amazed at how fast they could run in a slightly bent position as they moved through the tunnels. At times when a tunnel opened up, they could move even faster. They still managed to travel a great distance in both positions. Caleb figured their speed and ability to jump meant that the gravity in Boardland didn't have as much effect on real people as drawings. After all, Boardland was for some reason created for drawings.

When they approached the opening Nadie had identified, they came to a place where a tunnel turned up to their right. Nadie, who was leading, immediately ran up. Again, the opening was covered by bluish grass. Nadie gently pushed it away as she held her breath trying to avoid the inevitable chalk dust that followed. When she looked out she realized they had come up in the middle of a large meadow. She cautiously looked around before climbing out.

"I don't see anything but a large meadow bordered by forest," she reported.

"Any sign of Abstractshire?" Caleb asked as he poked through.

Nadie, who turned as she looked in all directions, replied, "Nope, but I was sure the map showed this tunnel came up near it."

Carona, who followed Caleb, noted that the meadow they'd just climbed into looked a lot like the one she had drawn on the blackboard. Even the wildflowers she'd drawn looked the same as these. "Do you think my meadow ended up in two places in Boardland?" she asked.

"That's highly unlikely," Caleb replied. "However, anything is possible here, even duplicates I guess."

"That sure would complicate things if an artist's drawing could produce duplicates," Nadie shared.

"Yeah, you wouldn't know if you were coming or going or if the drawing you were talking to was the same one you'd just met. Speaking of deja vu," Caleb noted.

As Caleb spoke the Illuminator's light suddenly dimmed. Before they knew what was happening they felt themselves being lifted into the sky. Caleb could hear Carona screaming as he realized they'd been snatched and lifted up by large raptor type claws. He was clutched in one and Nadie and Carona in the other. As he leaned back and looked up he saw a massive creature, half bird and half dragon, with large kite-like wings waving above them.

"What's happening to us?" he heard Nadie yell.

"I don't know, but I sure hope the thing's not hungry," Caleb yelled back.

"A light lunch would be nice," a slow deep voice replied.

"Did you hear that?" Nadie exclaimed.

"I did!" Carona bleated out.

Caleb, trying to get a look at the creature's head, turned toward his sisters, and yelled, "I think it was the creature. I think it can talk!"

"Then say something to it," Nadie shouted. "You have the loudest voice!"

"Where are you taking us?" Caleb yelled.

"To my tree, like I said. A light lunch would be nice," the voice came back.

"But we're here to help you. We're the Talbots the Legend talked about. We're here to save you!" Caleb yelled.

"Humm. It looks to me like you're the ones that need saving, not me," the deep voice replied.

Caleb wasn't sure what to say next but he had little doubt that they'd all soon be lunch if he couldn't talk the creature out of eating them. "We're not from Boardland!" he yelled back.

"I was wondering why you all felt so...clean," the creature replied.

"We're not a drawing. We're real people who came to Boardland to help you get rid of the General," he continued.

"The General, huh, he never bothers me. He and his Fingers can't fly. They can't even leave the ground," they heard the creature say followed by what sounded like a deep laugh.

Caleb noticed that they were headed towards a jagged mountain range about two miles in front of them. "Can't you land so we could talk?" Caleb yelled.

"That would be the nice thing to do," Caleb heard a soft comforting voice say.

"Oh, do you have to get involved with my lunch, Gleam?" the creature replied as they noticed a bright light just below them.

"The Talbots are here to help us. It would be wrong to harm them," Gleam replied as the light grew even brighter almost blinding them.

"Now I can't see," the annoyed creature exclaimed. "All right, I'll land," he said and glided slowly towards the shore of a little green lake.

"Thank you," Gleam replied as the bright light dimmed and followed them down.

"Gleam, are we glad to see you!" exclaimed Nadie.

They could make out Gleam's angelic form and face. "I'm sorry you had to meet Swoop in this way. He usually is better behaved," she sang out.

"I didn't know they were friends of yours. Strangers can often make a good meal," Swoop replied.

"The Illuminator doesn't want you eating the drawings or other visitors. He will allow you to grab an occasional Finger if you really need to eat something, but this you know."

Swoop who displayed the look of a young child being scolded. replied, "You're right! But they lied to me and told me they were the legendary Talbots. So, like the Fingers, they deserved to be eaten."

"But they are the Talbots, and all our hope of ridding Boardland of the General rests with them. I know he and his Fingers can't bother you but wouldn't this be a better place if he was gone? Don't you have some flying friends who are Scribbles?"

"Now that you mention it, I do," Swoop replied while stretching out his wings as though he were about to fly.

"You should be helping them, not annoying them," Gleam continued.

"Yes, Swoop. I'm Caleb and these are Nadie and Carona Talbot. We really could use all the help we can get."

"I'm still hungry. Can I go now Gleam?" Swoop asked.

"Only if you promise to help the Talbots when they ask for it," she replied.

Swoop flapped his kite-like wings several times in frustration. "Yes, yes, I will help them but only because you asked."

"And you'll be polite to them and do what they say?" Gleam asked.

"If that's what you want. Can I go now?"

"Of course," Gleam said with a beautiful smile that seemed to fill the sky.

"Then I'm off," Swoop said as his mighty wings lifted him into the sky. "It was nice meeting you three Talbots. Just call my name and if I'm near I'll come," he yelled back.

"I wonder who the artist was that drew Swoop?" Carona thought out loud.

"He did appear rather suddenly not too long ago," answered Gleam, "but he usually is much better behaved. He doesn't like the General. Since the General and his Fingers haven't been able to trap him, he's not very concerned about the other atrocities the General commits. By the way, where were you three going when Swoop got hold of you?"

"We thought we'd taken the right tunnel from the General's castle to Abstractshire but we came up in a meadow nowhere near the shire," Nadie reported.

"Then I take it you've had a chance to see where the General lives and also met the Tunnelers," Gleam replied.

"Yes to both. We can see why he's so feared by the citizens of Boardland and we've developed a positive relationship with Groff and the Tunnelers," said Caleb.

"Then it sounds like you're making good progress towards developing your plan. Now you also have Swoop as an ally," Gleam mentioned.

"I hope so," replied Carona, "But I don't know how much he's going to help us."

Gleam evoked a slight but musical laugh.

"Oh Carona, I'm sure he'll help when he's needed. As for Abstractshire, you are very near to it. If you follow that chalky yellow road, at the speed you can travel, you should be able to get there in no time. Now I must be going," Gleam added as she floated upward towards the Illuminator.

"Thank you for your help!" Carona shouted.

"I'm just happy that Swoop didn't take us further out of our way," Nadie exclaimed.

"Or had us for lunch!" Carona added.

"And I'm glad that Gleam showed up when she did. But when Swoop had us in his claws I kept feeling like I belonged in the sky," Caleb said.

"I did too," Nadie noted. "I felt that if Swoop had dropped me I wouldn't have fallen. It was really weird."

Carona thought for a moment then said, "Maybe it has something to do with our powers in Boardland. Maybe we have another power we don't know about yet."

"You could be right," Caleb agreed as he looked at the map. "I'm still not sure what these lines are in the sky. The ones on land are roads and trails, while the ones underground are tunnels dug by the Tunnelers. But the ones in the sky...I really don't know."

"I don't know either but for now I think we should be heading for Absractshire before it gets too late and we need to get back to our house in the Forest of Memories," Nadie suggested as Caleb took another look at the map.

"I see the road that Gleam said we should take. She's right. Abstractshire isn't that far. We'd better get going," said Caleb.

As they ran, Caleb felt he was actually getting used to Boardland. Even though the surroundings were strange, if not weird, he kind of enjoyed the variety and nature of the drawings. Funny trees, some bent and twisted, purple and red mountains that looked incomplete, buildings which seemed to wobble as if at any moment they'd fall, all somehow seemed to make sense to him. He didn't consider himself an artist much less an art critic, but he felt he could appreciate each drawing for what the artist was attempting to do. There was beauty and purpose in even the most incomprehensible Scribble. Suddenly he realized that Nadie and Carona had slowed down.

"Why are you slowing?" he asked.

"We hear a noise like thunder ahead of us," Nadie replied as they all slowed to a stop.

Looking up the road they could see a large cloud of yellow chalk-dust rising while the noise grew louder. Caleb recognized the sound as similar to the noise the horses made when they were hiding near the General's castle.

"Quick!" he yelled, "Run over to those bushes on our left. I think it's the General's horsemen! No time to cover our footprints!"

Together, they lunged towards the bushes, raising a cloud of blue, green, and yellow dust that quickly settled on and around them. Peering out between the branches, they saw several Scribbles and a Scrawl running and bounding up the road. Some looked like letters, others like various likenesses of animals or people, all difficult to differentiate. Right behind them were eight Fingers smudging every Scribble they could reach as they rode through them. The smudged drawings were left wiggling on the roadside, damaged just enough to prevent them from getting away.

"Caleb," Carona whispered. "We have to do something. We can't let them destroy those poor drawings!"

Caleb quickly opened the map.

"I see there is a tunnel just down the road. I'll get their attention, lead them away, and then hide in the tunnel. You both stay here. If I don't come back for you, then run back to the Forest of Memories and we'll meet at Nadie's house."

"That's too dangerous," Nadie replied. "There are too many of them on horseback and they may be able to catch you!"

"I have to try," Caleb called back as he ran a-ways through the bushes. He popped out just in front of the horsemen, waving his arms and frightening the front three horses. Three Fingers were thrown to the ground as their horses bolted off in different directions. Immediately Caleb started running down the road with the five remaining Fingers riding close behind as the Scribbles scattered into the bushes.

At first Caleb out distanced the riders but soon he found that a couple of the mounted Fingers were beginning to advance on him. When he glanced back a second time he could see two of the riders pulling out ropes and swinging lassoes over their heads. He knew he was fast but somehow those two riders had unbelievably quick horses. The artists that drew them must have drawn Kentucky derby winners, he thought. He could almost feel a horse's breath on the back of his neck and knew he had to do something quickly or possibly get roped.

Jump he thought. He knew he could go at least twenty to thirty feet into the sky, but then he'd have to come down. It was his only chance. Just as the closest rider was preparing to throw his rope, Caleb thought to himself 'high in the sky' and threw up his arms and leaped up off his right foot as hard as he could. For a moment he could see the two horsemen keeping up just below him and knew he'd come down right between them. But then instead of falling back down he began to climb higher into the air. Soon the horsemen, who had stopped, were just specks below him. His arms were still thrown forward as if to get the highest possible jump, but instead he was flying like superman into the clouds.

"What's happening?" he thought, as he twisted his body slightly to the right only to find it caused him to turn.

"To the left," he told himself as he twisted, feeling his flight direction turn him to the left.

He knew that flying for humans like this was impossible, yet there he was, flying circles around a small cloud. This is unbelievable. It obviously must be a special gift that they had in Boardland. This would make it almost impossible for General Eraser to capture them, he thought. He knew he needed to fly back and tell Nadie and Carona. As he started to make a large circle back he felt something pushing his arms and side, making him turn in a much smaller circle. Yet there was nothing but sky around him.

Caleb was heading back where he had just come from but couldn't figure out what made him turn so sharply. He decided to make another large circle and head back behind him. Again, something pushed against him and made him turn back more abruptly. Then he made a quick right turn and flew off in that direction, which worked for the first couple hundred feet. Again, he felt himself being pushed around in the direction he'd just come from. "This is crazy!" he thought. He could fly certain directions and go up and down but when he tried to fly outside of what seemed to be a limited flight lane, he couldn't do it.

Confused, Caleb decided to fly back to where he'd left his sisters. As he approached he could make out the bushes on the side of the road where they'd hidden. He didn't see any horsemen or Fingers so he slowly descended to the road. He immediately ran over to the bushes but found no one. He looked down at the chalky ground and saw two sets of footprints heading back down the road away from the direction he'd led the riders. Unfortunately, he also noticed that several of the horses must have turned around and their tracks were now following Nadie and Carona's footprints.

He started after them not knowing whether he should run or fly. If he flew could he fly in the direction of the road on which his sisters were running? Then he remembered the map Mr. Abe had given him. He quickly opened it and for the first time understood what the strange lines in the sky must represent. The map displayed all of Boardland's trails and roads and even had most of the Tunnelers' underground tunnels marked.

"So," he thought, "the lines in the sky must be sky trails!"

They now had the power to fly in Boardland but they were limited to flying only where the sky trails led.

"Weird" he thought.

Yet Boardland was a world of drawings and art. Even with art there are certain rules and techniques that must also be followed to gain the proper perspective and dimensions for a drawing. Apparently, when it came to the third dimension of depth within the sky, there were certain rules that must be followed. That could be the reason for the sky lines on Mr. Abe's map. They were the parameters of flight that had to be followed.

Caleb quickly perused the map to see if any of the sky trails were above the road. He noted that there was a sky trail marked just to the right of the road. He could fly after them and see what was happening.

Another thought came to him: "Why didn't Mr. Abe just tell us about the tunnels and sky trails? Why did he make us find out about them ourselves? And how did he even know about them in the first place when obviously the General had no idea? Enough of this, I have to find my sisters!"

He folded the map and jumped into the sky only to find that after a nice twenty-five feet high jump up, he landed back on the ground.

"Now what's happening? What did I do wrong? I'm standing under the sky trail. Why can't I go up into the sky again?"

Just as he had the last thought his body seemed to lift slightly off the ground.

"That's it! I need to think what I thought before I flew last time!"

Caleb began to run. He threw his arms into the air as he jumped off his right foot and thought, "high in the sky." Immediately, he lifted up and began to fly.

He followed the road for several minutes as he watched it wander towards Abstractshire. He stayed high but would often descend to check the road for Nadie's and Carona's footprints. Soon he noticed a cloud of chalky yellow dust rising in the road in front of him. He caught sight of two Fingers rapidly riding along the road. In front of them were Nadie and Carona. Caleb figured they must be the same Fingers riding the fast two horses that almost roped him. He knew he had to act quickly as both riders were swinging their lassoes. But how could he let his sisters know that they could simply fly away? Maybe he could swoop down and grab them, but then how could he possibly be strong enough to lift them up much less fly away with them.

"You can grab and lift them you know," a voice said quickly.

Caleb turned his head in all directions trying to figure out where the high pitched fast speaking voice had come from.

"Is that you Gleam?" he asked

No one answered for a moment, and then he heard the voice again. "You don't have much time, hurry, and pick them up."

Assuming it must be Gleam, Caleb answered. "I'm not strong enough for that, I'll drop them."

"No you won't. You have the strength, and I'm not Gleam!" the high-pitched voice rapidly called out. "I'm Spark. I help Flicker and Gleam, but enough of that. You have the strength so save them before the Fingers tie them up."

"If you say so," Caleb said knowing he had no other options. Immediately he descended just over the top of the riders and grabbed each sister by the arm. He shot back up making a quick circle that had him flying above the road in the opposite direction. To his amazement his sisters felt much lighter than he had expected. They both screamed not knowing what had happened to them.

"It's me, Caleb!" he yelled as he saw the Fingers staring up in disbelief.

"Put us down!" he heard Nadie yell. "What are you doing to us?"

"Saving you, I think!" he yelled back. "When it's safe, I'll land!"

Because of the speed he was flying he soon landed near the spot in the road where they had first hidden from the horsemen. He descended and gently placed Nadie and Carona on the road. As he cautiously glanced around, Caleb noticed that the Scribbles that had been chased and partly smudged were gone.

"What are you...how did you...you were flying!" Nadie stuttered.

"Yes, yes and you can too. Are you both all right?" he asked.

His sisters stared at him not knowing what to say. "You grabbed me and flew with me!" Carona finally bleated back.

Trying to calm his sisters a smiling Caleb said, "It appears to be another special power we have in Boardland even though I still can't believe it!"

Trying to catch her breath, Nadie replied, "We can fly too?"

"Yes, you just have to throw your arms into the air as you jump and think, 'high in the sky', and then you fly like Superman! Pretty good, huh!"

Both girls looked at each other in disbelief.

"But how could you possibly pick both of us up at once? Nadie asked. "Are you Tarzan too?"

Caleb thought for a moment.

"That I can't figure out," he said. "All I remember is a high-pitched, quick-speaking voice named Spark telling me that I had enough strength to do it. Looks like whoever he was turned out to be right!"

"Spark?" asked Nadie.

"Said he was a helper for Flicker and Gleam, and then disappeared."

"This place is amazing. Just as we're about to get roped by two Fingers on horseback Caleb flies in and pulls us into the air because a voice named Spark said he could! Go figure!" Nadie exclaimed.

"We should be traveling on to Abstractshire," said Caleb. "We need to rally the drawings and get their support."

"Did you really mean it when you said we could fly just by jumping, throwing our arms up, and thinking "high in the sky?" Carona asked.

"I think so. That's what happened to me. But I have to warn you that you can't just fly anywhere you want."

"Why, Caleb?" Carona inquired.

"Remember those lines that are drawn on the map Mr. Abe gave us? They turned out to be sky trail lines that limit us to flying just in the corridor of sky they're drawn in."

Wrinkling her nose up in disbelief Nadie replied, "Sky trails that have to be followed?"

"Yep! If you try to fly somewhere else, something simply shoves you back into the boundaries. The good news is that we can still fly almost anywhere since there are sky trail lines all over the map."

"Is there one that lets us fly from here to Abstractshire?" Carona asked.

"The sky trail I just flew in will take us back in the direction we were originally running and right to Abstractshire."

"Just be careful. It takes some time
to get used to."

"Then I want to fly right now!" Carona yelled as she started running.

"Just be careful. It takes some time to get used to and remember to think 'high in the sky!'" Caleb yelled after her.

As Carona threw her arms up and jumped, she began to float slowly up. Watching Carona seemed to excite Nadie, for she too was soon running and jumping into the air. Caleb couldn't help but smile as he saw both his sisters' delight as they flew toward a low cloud. Soon he joined them above the road leading to Abstractshire.

After a few minutes of watching his sisters turn small loops and undertake other flying maneuvers, Caleb spotted Absractshire. Immediately he gestured indicating that they land on the road below, not wanting to frighten the drawings by landing on their town square. He could tell that both Nadie and Carona would much rather continue flying when they both nodded 'no' as he persisted in pointing down. Finally, they all landed just outside of town.

"I think that alone was worth the visit to Boardland!" Nadie exclaimed.

Carona, who looked like she was about ready to jump back into the sky, added, "I felt like a bird only I didn't even have to flap my wings!"

"I enjoyed it too. I can't figure out how or why we can fly, but I guess it's one of our special perks!" said Caleb. "But now we have a dictator to rid Boardland of so we need to see if Abstractshire will help us with our plan."

Chapter Seven

Abstractshire and Primitivepality

As they walked into the most dilapidated town they'd ever seen, Scribbles and Scrawls began running, bouncing or rolling in every direction. The Talbots could see panic and fear in the eyes of each drawing that had them. The drawings were suddenly being visited by the most perfect renditions of real people they'd ever seen, drawings who would never bother to visit or be allowed in Abstractshire. Surely this must be some kind of terrible plot by General Eraser to harm them.

As Caleb, Nadie, and Carona entered the center of town, they stopped. Just about everything that could move had disappeared into some kind of shelter, habitation, or sanctuary. Certainly the young artists who drew the inhabitants and structures in this town were the only ones who knew what their drawings meant. Yet, the Talbots understood that even these were worthy since they represented how the young artist interpreted his personal thoughts through art.

"We better think of a way to put them at ease," Carona suggested. "I don't like causing them so much fear and pain."

"Let me try," said Nadie.

"Go for it," Caleb replied.

With a broad smile on her face Nadie spoke loudly and slowly. "You have all heard of the 'Legend' and have lived for the day when three real people would come to Boardland and save you from General Eraser. We're here to tell you that the time has come and the time is now. We are the three, real people you've been waiting for. We are the Talbots of your Legend. We believe that all drawings, no matter how they were drawn or what they look like, have a right to exist peacefully in Boardland. We've come to Abstractshire to ask you to help us develop a plan to get rid of the General. We're here for your help and support. If you touch us, you'll feel no chalk." Nadie stopped and looked around.

Caleb noticed some movement from under a porch attached to a small house to his right. Down the road he saw a Scribble of a snowman with a carrot for a nose peeking out from behind a wilted tree. Soon he disappeared.

"I don't think they believe us," said Carona. "There has to be something we could do to get them to believe us."

"We could fly," Nadie exclaimed. "I'm sure neither the General nor his Fingers can do that!"

"That's true," Caleb replied, "But don't forget about the General's spies Mr. Abe told us about. They may think we're just trying to trick them into coming out so we can smudge them. After all they have been living in fear and have had drawings they know smudged and erased, almost every night."

Nadie shook her head. "This is going to be harder than I thought."

"Could you use my help?" they heard a familiar voice say as Spring bounded out from behind some debris.

"Spring! What are you doing here?" Nadie asked. "I thought you were back in the Forest of Memories."

"I was, but when Curly told me that you were heading to Abstractshire, I thought I could help. After all I did live here for a long time."

Caleb sighed in relief as he said, "We sure could. We can't seem to get the inhabitants to trust us even though we reminded them about the Legend."

"They've learned to trust no one. Some of them have even been tricked by other Scribbles and have been erased. But they all know me and I think I can get them to be less suspicious."

"They have to let us help them," said Nadie, "Please make them listen, Spring."

Spring bounced several times then began yelling so most of Abstractshire could hear. "What they told you is true. They are the Talbots and they are here to help you. They've even spent time with Mr. Abe who knows for sure they are Caleb, Nadie, and Carona, from the Legend. Send someone out to touch them like I'm touching Nadie right now," Spring said as she reached out and patted Nadie on her side. "All of you who are looking can see that she has no dust. They are real people. Can't you tell they are the most perfect people you have ever seen...even better than those who live in Realtown?"

Suddenly several Scribbles appeared while keeping their distance. One of them moved forward cautiously. The drawing was definitely a sketch of an older boy who was quite twisted and bent. He moved forward keeping Spring between them and himself.

"I thought you'd be the first to take a look, Sketchard," Spring said with a bound and a giggle. "You've always been my most curious friend."

"Is what you're saying true, Spring, that they are the...Legend?" Sketchard asked.

"Have I ever lied to you?" she replied sharply.

Sketchard stopped and took three steps back. "Now don't get me wrong, Spring. You know I'm curious but you also know I've survived many years in Boardland by being cautious."

"And you're one of my smartest friends, too. Yes, they are the Talbots from the Legend!"

Suddenly, Sketchard seem concerned and distracted backing up as he looked down the road behind them. Instantly Spring was alarmed by his actions and turned to look. Caleb, Nadie, and Carona did the same.

Walking down the road into town were the Scribbles that looked like the same ones they'd seen being chased by the horsemen. Several of them were straining as they pulled a wagon with large wheels that were squarer than round. Inside the wagon were the Scribbles that had been smudged by the Fingers and left wiggling on the roadside. Several were still wiggling with arms, legs or other portions on their figures damaged or missing. Upon seeing the Talbots the procession stopped.

Carona was the first to notice the pain and fear on the faces of the Scribbles in the wagon. Immediately tears came to her eyes. Nadie and Caleb also realized that all the drawings in Boardland had emotions and feelings just like the living entities they were supposed to represent. For the first time the Talbots understood exactly how much actual suffering was being caused in Boardland by the General and his Fingers.

With tears streaming down her face, Carona began walking towards the wagon. As she approached, she took off her backpack. The Scribbles were either too scared or too tired to move. Carona pulled something from her backpack and walked up to a stick figure sketch of a little girl in the wagon whose right arm and leg had been smudged to the point of being virtually gone. The little girl was scared and in pain but seeing the tears and comforting smile that Carona displayed caused her to sit still. Carona stepped forward with a light-yellow piece of chalk and proceeded to draw an arm and a leg over the smudged ones. The little girl immediately smiled and stood up.

Caleb and Nadie were amazed. How could that happen? Did the colored chalk they'd been given by Manny have the power to draw and fix drawings in Boardland?

Everyone else in Abstractshire stood silently in awe. No one seemed to believe their eyes until Carona also drew an ear and front leg back on a Scrawl that appeared to be a rabbit. She then decided to help them out by making the square wheels on the wagon round. This made the wagon roll forward a yard or more on its own since it had been coming down the road into town.

First Sketchard ran forward as Spring began to bounce around singing out "Finally we'll be free. The Eraser is going to flee. The Fingers will follow. We'll be merry tomorrow, and we'll all live happily!"

Almost in unison a loud yell and cheering could be heard throughout the town. The Scribbles that could began to applaud and moved forward to surround the Talbots and the wagon. Soon, with Spring and Sketchard leading, everyone was chanting, "Talbots! Talbots! Talbots."

Carona stood still not sure whether she should laugh or cry. Caleb and Nadie waved and smiled too, not sure what they should do next.

Finally, after what seemed like a respectable amount of time of cheering, Caleb raised his hand and yelled out, "Please listen! Please listen!" To his surprise everyone stopped at once and stared at him in anticipation.

"As the Legend states, we've been brought to Boardland to help save you from the General's cruel dictatorship. Besides being real people, we have been discovering the special powers we have in this land to help us as we devise a plan to rid you of this menace. As you can see one power we have is to fix smudged drawings and perhaps draw new ones. We are still learning about your land, our powers, and the General. But if we are to help you, you'll need to be brave enough to help us when we finally implement our plan. Are you willing to help us?"

Immediately Caleb heard them yelling, "Yes!" and chanting "Talbots" all over again.

Sketchard was now standing next to him patting him on the back. Caleb wasn't sure whether Sketchard was simply double checking to make sure he was real using the chalk test or congratulating him for being their savior and friend.

"Whatever your plans, we will do anything you ask," said Sketchard.

"Then you must be prepared to act as soon as you receive our orders," Nadie exclaimed.

"What orders?" a familiar voice asked.

"Curly, where have you been? You've missed the most amazing thing!" Sketchard replied. "The Legend is for real, the Talbots are for real, and they have all kinds of powers with which to help us. Isn't that just amazing? After all these years we're finally going to be rid of the General!"

Looking a bit surprised, Curly said, "Yes, I knew they were here to help us and I'm so glad they have discovered their special powers. Please, Sketchard and Spring, tell me more."

As the townspeople celebrated over the arrival of the Talbots, Nadie and Caleb walked over to Carona who was standing near the cart.

"That was amazing, Carona. Whatever made you think you could fix smudged drawings with our colored chalk?" Nadie asked.

"I really didn't even think of anything except that I wanted to help them. When I saw the smudged chalk I just did what I usually do when I smudge it on the blackboard. I simply replace it with new chalk. That's all I did."

"Yeah, and maybe revealed the most important power we have in Boardland," added Caleb.

"You mean redoing drawings?" Nadie asked.

Caleb smiled and replied, "Not only redoing but possibly making new drawings of anything we might need."

"Wow, that would be a special gift!" said Nadie. "What if we drew a picture of an even larger eraser with long arms for erasing?"

"That could be a big part of our plan. If it worked we could erase the entire General's Finger soldiers," Caleb replied.

"And I could make all the Scribbles that have trouble moving or speaking better. Maybe then they would look real enough that even General Eraser would leave them alone," Carona added.

They all started laughing. The tension and stress that had been building in each of them as they struggled to find a solution momentarily broke free. All kinds of ideas for a plan to rid Boardland of the evil General swarmed through their heads. Suddenly Carona stopped laughing and looked down.

"What's the matter, Carona? Aren't you happy about being able to help the Scribbles?" Nadie asked.

Carona looked up. Her smile had been replaced with tears. "Yes, I'm happy, but I'm worried."

"About what?" Caleb asked.

"I don't think we should try to change the Scribbles, unless they've been smudged."

"Okay, why shouldn't we?" Nadie asked.

Taking a long deep breath Caleb answered, "I think I know why. It's because of the artists, the people whose ideas and talents created the drawings, isn't it?"

Carona looked at Caleb then nodded. "We'd be changing someone else's thoughts and feelings and how they expressed them in their drawings on the board. I don't think we have the right to do that."

"But you just changed some and look at the good you did," Nadie noted.

"Yes, Nadie, Carona did just that out of love and concern. But those Scribbles had been smudged and she just returned them to their original form. That's very different," Caleb concluded.

"I see what you mean. Yet, it would sure make life a lot easier in Boardland for many drawings if we could just touch them up a bit," Nadie replied.

"We need to think this over. We also need to get back to the house so we can be alone and find out to what extent we actually can use our chalk."

"I agree, Caleb. Now the Scribbles of Abstractshire know the Legend is real and they are willing to help us. Mr. Abe, Flicker, Gleam, and maybe even Swoop said they would help. Besides, we've discovered powers we have in Boardland that we could only have dreamed of a day ago. Now we have to start putting a plan together," said Nadie.

"Don't we still have to convince the drawings living in Realtown, Impressionville and Primitivepality that they need to help us?" Carona added.

"Yes, we should certainly try," Caleb replied. "It might be much harder convincing them to help since the General's plan is to only erase Abstractshire."

"That's true, but what if he changes his mind and afterwards wants to keep only the most perfect drawings in Realtown?" Nadie added.

"That could actually be what he plans to do in the future," Caleb replied. "If the drawings in Impressionville and Primitivepality could be convinced of that possibility, we might get them to support us. I see on the map we could swing by Primitivepality on our way back to the Forest of Memories, at least if we use the trails or roads."

"Sounds good to me," Nadie exclaimed. "But I think we should say goodbye to everyone, even Spring, Curly and Sketchard. I don't think they would be as welcomed in Primitivepality as they are here."

"They what?" the General yelled as he jerked back on the reins of the nearly perfect prancing black stallion he'd been riding just outside the castle grounds. "The Talbots were seen again. The Legend is definitely true?"

"General, General, they've been seen and chased and almost roped by several of our soldiers," Captain Thumb shot back while trying to calm the General down.

"Then why aren't they here, all tied up?"

"My General, they ran away."

"You mean they out ran our fastest horses?"

"Oh, no, General, our fastest riders almost caught them."

"Then how did they get away?"

"Just when our men were going to rope them, uh, they flew away," Captain Thumb reported as he prepared for the next verbal assault.

"What? They just grew wings and floated away?"

"Oh no, my General. The soldiers said they just jumped into the air and...then floated away."

"Absurd, impossible, nothing can go up into the sky in Boardland but birds and the Illuminator's helpers. You don't think the men mistakenly saw a beam or a ray floating by...do you?"

The Captain tried to figure out a way to escape the General's questioning and then replied, "That's possible, but they did say they looked like two girls and a boy. I'll double check and also talk with our spies."

"In the meantime, gather my soldiers. As soon as you can find out where these Talbots or whatever they are will be, I personally plan to capture them. That should put an end to all this nonsense. Now hurry, I'm still going to erase Abstractshire in three days!"

The Talbots decided to move cautiously along a trail to Primitivepality that, according to the map, passed through a large wooded area. Staying as much as they could out of sight and being as inconspicuous as possible was the best option. Carona did suggest it would be much more fun to use a tunnel, but Nadie and Caleb agreed that they should only be used in an emergency.

While they carefully walked along the trail, Caleb, who was walking just ahead of Nadie and Carona, still couldn't believe where they were or why they had been the people in the Legend. How had they been picked years ago to save Boardland? What made them so special? If it was their destinies, just how were they going to get rid of the General and his tyrannical hold on Boardland? Sure, now they had some unbelievable powers and even drawings that would help them, but what about General Eraser? Surely he had powers, too. What were they besides his gang of Fingers, his massive body, and his ability to erase? Could Caleb really be sure he and his sisters could handle the General and his Fingers without themselves becoming casualties?

The more Caleb evaluated their situation, the more he was convinced that they still needed more answers. Gleam and Flicker could help, if they were allowed to, but he had no way of contacting them. The only other one who might know was Mr. Abe. Caleb figured they needed to visit him as soon as possible.

Just as Caleb decided to talk to his sisters, he realized they'd been walking under a shadow even though the sky was cloudless above the few fir trees.

"Do you need any help, yet?" a loud deep voice bellowed out.

Immediately they all stopped in their tracks and looked up. Floating above them through the openings in the trees they could see two large kite-like wings.

"Swoop!" a grinning Carona yelled out.

"Remember me?" he answered back.

"Of course we remember you!" Nadie called back. "You're the one who was taking us out for lunch...literally!"

"Yes, that was me. I'm sure you would have been tasty."

"What do you want?" Caleb called back.

"Gleam told me I should check with you to see if you needed any help yet?"

Caleb thought for a moment. "Thank you, not right now. Will you be seeing Gleam soon?" he yelled up.

"I don't know. She always seems to find me. I wish she'd mind her own business sometimes."

"If you do find her, please tell her that we need to speak with her," Caleb yelled.

"Now I'm a messenger pigeon. Okay, if I see her."

"Be sure to stay nearby. We'll need your help very soon," Nadie called up.

"Where are you flying to now?" a curious Carona yelled.

"Oh, I plan on having a Finger for lunch. There are a bunch of them just up ahead hiding in the trees. I guess they're probably waiting for you."

"There are Fingers ahead waiting for us?" Caleb yelled back.

"Yep, ten of them on horseback. Maybe I'll have a horse for my meal today."

Caleb, unsettled by the information and trying to keep his head, yelled back, "That would be a great idea. We'll just wait here for a few minutes while you pick out the best one."

"Okay, I'll pick out a nice plump one...and, oh yeah, and chase the rest away so they won't stop you from going wherever you're going."

"We'd really appreciate that, Swoop," Caleb yelled.

As they watched Swoop fly on ahead of them, Nadie breathed a sigh of relief. "We were almost going to be guests in the General's dungeon! It's a good thing Swoop came along."

"We were sure lucky on that one, although I don't think Swoop has quite the right idea on how he can help us," Caleb replied.

Carona, deep in thought, asked, "I wonder how the Fingers knew where we were going so they could hide and wait for us?"

"Yeah, what's up with that?" Nadie added.

"The only way they would have known is if someone in Abstractshire told them," Caleb replied.

"Spies in Abstractshire?" Carona asked.

"It makes sense. If the General plans to erase it, then he probably needs someone on the inside to let him know what's going on. So, someone there must have overheard us as we talked about traveling to Primitivepality."

"They don't have cell phones here, do they?" Nadie asked.

"That I can't answer, but someone could have drawn one on the blackboard. Even some fourth graders use them."

Nadie shook her head, "Wow, a chalk land with cell phone communication towers!"

"Quick! Hide in those bushes to our right. I hear horses coming," Caleb exclaimed.

As they dove into some yellowish bushes and caused a small dust cloud to float up, four Fingers on horseback rode frantically by, not bothering to check out the rising dust.

"He got Corporal Pinky...and his horse! Stay in the trees and ride as fast as you can!" they heard the last horseman yell out.

As they slowly emerged from the bushes, Nadie announced, "That was too close, but it looks like Swoop got a meal. I think Carona was right, Caleb. Let's find a tunnel to follow."

Caleb unfolded the map and laid it across a fallen tree.

"Let's see, we should be about here on the trail and..."

"Right here, Caleb. There's a tunnel entrance!" an excited Carona exclaimed.

"I think you've got this map figured out better than I do, Carona. It looks like we need to go back down the trail about a block and then to our right to this small meadow."

Before Caleb could refold the map, both Nadie and Carona were running back along the trail. As he caught up he heard Nadie yell out. "You know, we could have flown to Primitivepality. I saw a sky trail on the map right above us."

"So did I, but with so many Fingers looking for us after our last near capture, they're probably watching the sky for us now too...and also for Swoop!"

"Good point, Caleb. I think I see the meadow through those trees," Nadie replied as she quickly shot to her right.

They spent several minutes searching the high meadow grass before Caleb stepped on a grassy area that felt firm. He felt around until he found a place to slide his fingers under something. Then he slowly lifted up a crude wooden door covered with grass.

"Thought there'd be a door this time since the opening was in the middle of a meadow. Let's get inside before someone spots us."

Carona, then Nadie dropped in before Caleb. Once again, the drop was about fifteen feet. Yet, to them, it seemed like stepping off a chair. Immediately their eyes became used to the purple glowing darkness. They started running along the tunnel which seemed to follow directly below the wooded trail they had been using. Within minutes Caleb figured they were close to Primitivepality and began slowing down to look for a tunnel that headed up. Except for the purple coloring their vision in the tunnel was probably as clear as the Tunnelers.

"To our left!" Caleb called out as he slowed down and moved up.

Caleb pushed his head up through some thick bushes and peered around before climbing out. The opening was covered with dense growth and surrounded by hundreds of small fir trees.

"This looks like the Christmas tree farm we went to three years ago when mom let us cut down our own tree," Carona exclaimed.

"It was probably drawn by some fourth grader who had also just visited a tree farm like we did," Nadie added. "All the trees are exactly the same and seem to be in rows."

Caleb, still cautious as he looked around, said, "Whoever it was sure had a lot of green chalk! Let's see if we can find a way out of this tree farm and discover where we are."

They all moved in the direction shown on the map. As soon as they emerged from the grove of trees, they were able to make out buildings in the distance.

"Wait a minute," Nadie whispered. "Quick, kneel down in the grass so we can't be seen."

Caleb, the tallest, poked his head up and looked over the high yellow grass. "Now I see it. A group of drawings is sitting on logs in a circle. They all look like they were drawn by someone who had just started taking drawing lessons, kinda messed up but definitely people."

"Looks like some of the inhabitants of Primitivepality are having some kind of gathering," Nadie noted as she was half standing.

Carona found she could stand straight up without being seen in the grass. "Let's sneak closer. Maybe we can find out what they're talking about."

"You mean snoop on them?" Nadie asked.

"Sure, just like we have to do with mother to find out what's going to happen to us next," Carona replied.

"I'm game," added Caleb, "We're good at this!"

The three of them crawled towards the circle trying not to stir up the grass's yellow chalk dust. Caleb led the way, taking them towards a few bushes that stood where the grass stopped just next to the drawings. A thick, short looking man wearing jeans, a dark blue T-shirt, and a baseball cap was speaking

"I don't know, Coal, what we should do. If the General destroys Abstractshire, that would be terrible. I know we're not supposed to interact with drawings from the other cities but I do have a few...well... friends in the Shire. I wouldn't want them to be erased!"

"I have to admit it too, Half Pint. I have let's say acquaintances there also. I know as the city leaders we're supposed to oversee Primitivepality for the General and keep everyone contained," replied a taller man in a dark suit who looked like he'd been entirely drawn with a charcoal pencil.

"You mean our job is to keep them manipulated, subjugated, and repressed for the General, or else!" shouted a girl.

The young girl was wearing a full red skirt decorated with small white circles and a bonnet that matched tied under her chin with a white bow.

"Shh, not so loud, Dot. A spy could hear us," cautioned Coal, who seemed to be the leader. "You know our real task is to keep everyone safe from the General's wrath. We're in a very precarious position. We all feel the same about his despotism, yet he does leave us alone while he races after Scribbles and Scrawls."

"Yes, I know. But why should they be sacrificed? Who made him king?" Dot replied in a softer tone.

"You know the answer to that. No one did. Being an eraser of his size and power put him in the position to take over. Then when those Fingers appeared out of nowhere he used those sneaky, smudging rascals as his henchmen. What are we supposed to do?"

"I know," Half Pint exclaimed. "Wait for the Talbots?"

"Yeah," replied Coal. "That legend has been around so long I think it's time we forget about it. It only keeps our hopes up and keeps us from doing something ourselves," Coal replied.

"Then we're back where we started," Dot sighed. "Then what can we do? Anybody else have an idea?"

At that point Caleb couldn't stop himself from getting involved. "I have a suggestion," he interjected as he stood up.

For a moment everyone in the circle turned and looked, then froze on the spot.

"Don't worry. I'm not a spy. I'm here to help you."

Finally, Coal spoke. "What are you doing here? You're from Realtown. If a Finger sees you here we'll all be in trouble. Go quick, leave!" he shouted as the rest of the drawings in the circle called out, "Leave, leave!"

"But I'm not from Realtown. I'm Caleb Talbot from the Legend. Mr. Abe can verify that for you if you want."

"Then you must be a spy!" someone shouted from the circle.

Caleb thought for a moment before replying. "No, I'm not. If I were I would have snuck off to report to the General how you really felt about him. Then, all of you would have been smudged for treason. But I didn't, because I'm not a drawing but a real person."

There was a noticeable gasp from the group. Caleb could tell that they still weren't sure what to do, but sensed that most of them would prefer to run back into the safety of their town and avoid any more contact with him.

Again, Coal spoke up. "This is nonsense. If you are Caleb Talbot, where are Nadie and Carona Talbot, huh?"

At that moment both of his sisters stood up. An even louder gasp could be heard.

"To answer your question, I'm Nadie and this is my sister, Carona Talbot!"

Caleb could see they were thoroughly confused. He knew he had to do something before they ran, so he moved slowly toward Coal, who was the closest, and touched him. Immediately Coal jumped away, and then stopped. He paused and looked curiously at Caleb. "Wait, everyone," he said calmly. "His hand was solid with no chalk!"

"It must be some kind of a trick," Half Pint interjected

"No, I don't think so," Dot replied as her curiosity moved her slowly towards Caleb.

Caleb stood still as she reached out her simple little hand and touched his cheek, then his shoulder. Caleb couldn't help but smile when Dot peered carefully into his eyes. A smile gradually emerged on her face too.

"He certainly isn't from Boardland. I think he's telling the truth. They can only be the Talbots, and they'll know what to do!"

Another gasp rose from the circle as Coal stepped towards Caleb.

"If you truly are the Talbots, how are you going to get rid of the General?"

Caleb knew he needed to choose his words carefully.

"We're not going to rid Boardland of the General."

Immediately another gasp was heard as Coal jumped back. "We and you along with the drawings from the other towns are going to do that together!"

"You mean we're all going to gang up on them?" Half Pint asked.

"Exactly" Caleb exclaimed. "The drawings in Abstractshire have already agreed to help us. Now if you also join us, we'll just need to get the support from Impressionville and Realtown."

"This plan of yours doesn't involve us getting erased, does it?" Coal asked.

"Not if it works the way we hope it will. I'm not going to tell you that something bad couldn't happen. It's possible, but we all have to take chances and make some sacrifices to bring down the General."

"What if we don't help? What if we just leave everything the way it is and go about our business?" Half Pint asked.

"Then you'll still have the General and his Fingers ruling over you. We will be gone and the Legend will be no more. In other words, there will be no second chance," Caleb explained.

"No second chance?" Dot asked.

"No second chance," Caleb loudly replied. "Besides, if the General erases everyone in Abstractshire because he feels they are terrible drawings, won't you be next? As you know he wants more room in Boardland for only the most real drawings. Primitivepality and Impressionville would likely be next. After all, you're far from being perfect."

"We're almost perfect and we haven't caused any trouble," Half Pint noted quickly.

"That's just it," Nadie replied. "You're almost perfect, but probably not perfect enough to meet the General's artistic standards."

"Nadie's right," Coal concluded. "We have no guarantees the General won't hunt us down next. This is our only chance, while the Talbots are here. Let the Legend be fulfilled!" he yelled as he threw his right hand into the air.

Everyone in the circle spontaneously shot their hands up and yelled "Let the Legend be fulfilled!"

"Now our job is to convince the rest of our friends in town to follow us," said Coal.

"I'm sure they'll all agree," Dot replied.

Half Pint, stepped into the middle of the circle, shot his hand up, and shouted,

"Let the Legend be fulfilled!"

Caleb, Nadie, and Carona felt immediate relief. Now they were assured, or as assured as they could be, that at least two of the four towns would do whatever their plan required.

"So, they're in Primitivepality?" the General replied as he finished combing his long black hair. He smiled at himself in the mirror and reached up to twist his moustache at both ends.

"Yes, my General. They seem to be going to each town, probably to collect intelligence and find out if they can get help...that is if the Legend it true."

"We must plan for the worst case. I have to assume the Legend is very true and, knowing the Legend, I have to believe that they're trying to develop a plan to destroy us! I'm actually sure that's their plan. Anyone who helps them should be smudged at once. Now they'll go to Impressionville and then to Realtown. Are all my troops gathered?"

"Yes, your Excellency, all but a few who are still on patrol or checking with our spies for information. Except for...ah..."

"Except for what you imbecile!"

"Corporal Pinky...and his horse," Captain Thumb said softly.

The General looked at him suspiciously. "You mean we're missing the Corporal?"

"Not really, we know who he's with."

Not being a patient man, the General shouted out, "Then where is he?"

"Swoop picked him up out of his patrol while they were setting a trap for the Talbots."

The General's face turned as red as the stripes on his uniform. "You mean Swoop is having lunch at my expense...again?"

"Probably, sir."

"He's eating my soldiers faster than I can promote them. Soon all my Fingers will be gone! I've got to find a way to erase that weird bird creature. You say he's eating the Corporal's horse too?"

"Apparently, but at least this should keep him satisfied for a while."

The General shook with rage. Chalk dust began to fill the room as the Captain began to cough.

"Prepare my men. We'll leave immediately. I have a plan that should put an end to this Talbot rebellion!"

Chapter Eight

Rockbound Valley

"I don't think we have enough time today to go to both Impressionville and Realtown," Nadie noted. "We'll need to seek the safety of the Forest of Memories and our house before dark."

"You're right," Caleb replied as he pulled out his map. "Looks like Impressionville is just over those hills," he said as he pointed to the west.

Half Pint moved towards Caleb. "It's not very far, and I'll be glad to show you the way."

"I thought you were going to talk to the people about joining us," stated Carona.

"Don't worry, Carona," said Coal. "Dot and I will head straight to town with the rest of the council to tell them the news about the Legend and get their support. Half Pint is right. It's getting more dangerous in Boardland every minute, and he can show you the best trails to keep you hidden.

"But Caleb," Carona added. "what about talking to Mr. Abe?"

"Yeah, we still need to do that. Since we'll be going to Realtown tomorrow, we can stop by and see him. He's probably the only one there who could convince the drawings of Realtown to support our plan."

"Just what is the plan?" they heard a familiar voice ask.

Nadie was the first to spot Curly coming out of the high meadow grass where they had once stood.

"Curly, what are you doing here?" Half Pint asked.

"After the Talbots left us in Abstractshire I became concerned. Even though they have some special powers I thought they might need my help to show them around."

"Special powers?" Half Pint asked.

"Yes," Caleb replied. "As we've traveled around Boardland, I've learned that we can run as fast as the General's best horses, as well as fly, with certain restrictions."

Half Pint looked pleasantly surprised as did Coal and Dot.

"You never told us that!" said Coal.

"We would have told you when we finalized our plan," Caleb replied.

"That will certainly be useful information to use when we ask the rest of the drawings to support you," Coal replied.

"You're right, Coal," said Caleb. "I should have mentioned that earlier."

"Then you don't have a final plan?" asked Curly.

"We're just gathering the last pieces of information we'll need to prepare the plan. We will let all of you know what you each need to do when that happens," Caleb replied.

Half Pint walked over to Curly. "I know you mean well, but you're endangering us and yourself by being so close to our town. If you're spotted, the General will surely erase you. Besides, I'm going to guide them."

Curly looked at everyone, smiled and said, "Then you'd better be on your way. I know Half Pint knows Boardland as well as I do. I'll go back to Abstractshire and await your instructions."

"We do appreciate your putting yourself at risk to help us, Curly," said Carona.

"Anything I can do to help," Curly replied as he bounded into the high meadow grass scaring up a bird that looked something like a quail.

"He sure took a chance by coming here," Coal mentioned. "Anyway, you'd better be heading to Impressionville while we make sure all of Primitivepality is with us!"

Half Pint immediately threw his arm forward like a charging cavalry officer and trotted off towards the west, his short, stout legs not hindering him at all.

"I assume that means we should follow," Nadie said with a smile.

"It may be at a slower pace than we're used to but at least we will be taking the safest route," Carona agreed as she began to giggle.

"I really wish Gleam or Flicker would return to help us," Caleb whispered to his sisters. "They could help us finalize our plans with their knowledge of Boardland."

"Besides they said they would help if we wanted them too," Nadie whispered back.

"That's true," Carona added. "I always had the feeling they wanted us, because of the Legend, to make all the decisions."

"I don't know why the Great Illuminator doesn't just shut off all the sunlight to Boardtown or blind General Eraser with a brilliant ray from his sun. That would put an end to his dictatorship," shared Caleb.

"I don't think he works that way," said Carona. "Besides, I still think Room 7 has some control over the light in Boardland."

Nadie whispered back, "If he could they wouldn't need the Legend...and the Talbots!"

"And we'd be safe at home," noted Carona.

"Yeah, with Mom and her new boyfriend, Garth, sending us to our rooms whenever he decided to visit!" an obviously annoyed Nadie replied.

After jogging along behind Half Pint for several miles, over forested hills, they started to descend onto a large grassy valley where Half Pint stopped abruptly.

"What's the matter?" Caleb asked. "Are we close?"

"We're just a couple of miles away but we have to pass through Rockbound Valley, and I don't like it. It doesn't feel right," Half Pint replied.

Caleb, easily peering over the top of Half Pint's head, looked out at the open meadowy valley. It was engulfed on both sides by sharp rocky ridges then emptied into a thick forest that continued beyond. "I see what you mean. Can't we go around?"

"Not unless you're willing to lose an hour of daylight," Half Pint said as he turned toward Caleb.

"If we do that we might as well head back to the safety of our house. The Illuminator's light will be out by then," shared Nadie.

"Then we'd better run through the valley as fast as we can," a concerned Caleb replied.

Half Pint immediately raised his hand up into a position that seemed to indicate, "stop", before the Talbots could move forward. "Let me go first to check things out. I'll stop just before the forest and wave my hand if it's safe for you to follow."

"You know Boardland much better than we do so we'll wait for your signal. Just be careful," Caleb replied.

Half Pint smiled uneasily then started jogging down the remainder of the hill and across the open valley. He paused about every hundred feet and looked around, then continued.

"I hope everything is all right," said Carona as they all waited expectantly.

"I'm sure it is," Nadie replied, "He's almost across."

They watched as Half Pint stopped a couple hundred feet from the other end of the valley then waved his hand.

"Looks like everything's okay, but we'd be wise to move fast," Caleb said, and following Half Pint started jogging down the hill.

Half way across the valley Caleb noticed some movement coming from the forest in front of Half Pint. Immediately, several Fingers on horseback sprang from its shadows completely cutting Half Pint's escape route off. They pulled him up onto one of the horses and rode back. The Talbot's heard him yelling, "Run, Run," as he wiggled trying to get free.

"We better head back fast!" Caleb exclaimed.

As they turned, they saw ten more Fingers on horseback along with about twenty others on foot charging them from the very hill on which they'd once stood. Looking back, they noticed about the same number emerging from the forest's shadows. There in the lead was none other than the massive General Eraser himself riding on his equally imposing black stallion.

"We're trapped!" Caleb yelled out.

"Look!" Carona exclaimed as she pointed towards the forest where Half Pint had been taken. "They caught Curly too!" Sure enough, there stood Curly surrounded by several Fingers.

"I say it's time to fly," Nadie yelled.

"I sure hope there's a sky trail above us," Caleb answered as they all started running to gather speed for their jump.

"We've got them now!" the General's deep raspy voice bellowed out. "Surround them! No wait. They're going to try to fly away, but not from me!" he exclaimed as he jumped from his horse.

Luckily, a sky trail was above them and the Talbots were just beginning to gain some altitude when the General began to spin in circles pounding rapidly on his eraser like chest. Immediately a thick white chalk dust cloud began to rise, engulfing Rockbound Valley and the sky above.

The first thing the Talbots noticed was the complete lack of visibility. They couldn't see any land markings to guide their flight. At the same time the great cloud of chalk dust began to fill their lungs, making them gasp for air and their breathing almost impossible. In a moment they were coughing and choking.

"We have to land or we'll suffocate...and we'd better do it while we're still over the meadow grass or we could smash into the trees," gargled Caleb.

Not knowing where the ground was, they each hit the grass landing hard on their chests as they thumped then rolled over several times.

"Carona, are you all right?" Nadie called out.

"Yes, but my elbows and chin are scraped up."

"And I'm all right too, but be quiet or they'll find us," said Caleb.

"I'm sure I saw something fall, my General," yelled Captain Thumb, "just before the forest."

"Then my strategy worked. Even though the chalk dust doesn't bother us, I knew if they were the Talbots they would drown in it. Now everyone, find them. The dust should settle at any moment."

The three children lay silently in the grass, listening to the horses' hooves as the Fingers rode every which way around them. Caleb realized the danger of them being run over while the dust still hung low over the valley. He tried hard not to cough but knew he was about to pass out from lack of air. The smothered coughing sounds from Nadie and Carona had stopped. He hoped they could still breathe as he slipped into unconsciousness.

The chalk dust had finally settled as the General's men rode in circles around Rockbound Valley looking for the Talbots in the meadow grass.

"What do you mean you can't find them? They have to be here. You said you saw them drop from the sky!"

"Yes, my General," a very nervous Captain Thumb replied. "They must be here...in the grass. We'll continue our search. They could not have gotten by my men."

The Fingers continued their search to no avail. The Talbots were gone.

"Caleb, Caleb, wake up! You're going to be all right," Caleb heard a melodic voice sing out.

"What, who?" he mumbled as he tried to open his eyes. He could feel the chalk dust all over his face and arms. His nose was partly blocked and his eyes were watery as he tried to force the remaining dust from around his eyelids. "Where am I? Who are...?" Still in a daze, Caleb made out someone all in white with long white hair and bright red eyes looking down at him. "Flicker, is that you?"

"Yes, it's me. Swoop told me that you wanted to see me so I came looking for you. When I saw the General's dust storm over the valley I knew something bad was happening. He seldom uses that tactic unless he's really mad and determined so I knew the three of you were probably in trouble."

"Nadie and Carona, are they all right?" exclaimed Caleb.

"Oh yes," Flicker replied. "They'll be fine. They're just down in the tunnel."

"The tunnel?" Caleb asked as his eyes finally let him see the purple glow.

"How did we end up in a tunnel?"

"I arrived just as the three of you were trying to land. I knew, that since you are real, you wouldn't be able to survive the dust's blinding and choking features. Fortunately, there was a tunnel opening near where you fell. The Tunnelers say they don't really care what goes on above them, but they do. Groff usually has his men scouting around Boardland watching the movements of the General and his Fingers. He and some of his men had followed them, by tunnel of course, to this valley and figured they were up to no good so they hung around. I knew where a tunnel opening was in the valley so I lit up the opening as Groff and Satch quickly pulled the three of you in."

"Groff and Satch pulled us in?"

"Yes, Satch is still keeping watch on the General and his Fingers while Groff is attending to Nadie and Carona."

"I want to see them."

"By all means. They're just around the corner and closer to the tunnel opening since they were found and pulled in after you. I'll show you," Flicker replied as he moved down the tunnel.

As Caleb slowly stood up he put his hand on the side of the tunnel to steady himself.

"Wow, I'm really dizzy."

"Of course, you were unconscious for several minutes, unlike drawings which simply get disoriented and momentarily blinded by the dust," Flicker replied as Caleb wobbled along behind him.

"Caleb!" called out Nadie. "Are you okay?"

"Just a bit dizzy. How about both of you?"

"We're dizzy, too, and this chalk dust is miserable," Carona exclaimed. "I'm sure glad that Flicker and the Tunnelers found us. I think we would have suffocated."

"I agree", replied Nadie. "I couldn't breathe at all. I'm beginning to believe that the General can destroy us. He can harm us in ways much worse than chaining us in his dungeon."

"Me too," added Carona. "Even though the General's dungeon is the last place I want to be!"

A troubled Caleb agreed, "I think you're both right. We need to be very careful or this whole Legend thing can quickly get out of hand. I'm worried that we could be risking our lives."

"We did say we'd see this through. All the drawings are depending upon us!" Nadie exclaimed.

"We did, but up until now I looked upon it as an adventure not a life-threatening mission!" Caleb shared.

"We'll just have to have faith in ourselves and in the Great Illuminator, Mr. Abe, Flicker, and all the drawings who said they'd help us," Carona replied.

"We are their last hope," Nadie added.

"I guess we have to move on, but with extreme caution, and see what we can do," Caleb replied.

"And I, along with the rest of Boardland, will help all we can," Flicker exclaimed.

"Thanks, Flicker," replied Carona.

Deep in thought Caleb, asked, "You did see Curly surrounded by Fingers, didn't you?"

"Yes," Nadie replied, "just after they grabbed Half Pint!"

"I sure hope the General didn't erase them!" Carona added.

"I don't think he'd erase them, yet," said Flicker. "He's evil but also very calculating. He'll probably take them back to his castle and interrogate them. He'll want to know everything he can about the three of you."

Carona, looking worried, asked, "What will he do to them?"

"He's not a compassionate person. He'll probably smudge and even erase parts of them if they don't cooperate," Flicker replied.

"We can't let him do that," Caleb exclaimed. "We'll need to go back into his castle and save them. Like before, we'll use the next Recess to do it."

Flicker looked over at Caleb. "That won't be as easy the second time. He knows you entered his castle before during Recess and he'll expect you. He'll have traps set and probably hide Half Pint and Curly somewhere you'd never find them. I've heard his castle has several hidden chambers. Besides, today is Friday and the next Recess isn't for three days."

"Even if that's so, we still have to save them," Caleb replied.

"You're very brave, but another way to save them is to get rid of the General. Have you developed a plan yet?"

"We have support from the drawings of Abstractshire and Primitivepality. We were just heading to Impressionville when the General attacked us."

"That's very interesting," said Flicker.

"Why's that?" Nadie asked.

"If you were just at Primitivepality and immediately headed for Impressionville, how did the General know where to set a trap?"

"I was just thinking about that also," Caleb added. "We know the General has spies in Boardland and probably in Primitivepality, but how did he know where we were heading so soon?"

"Are there cell phones in Boardland?" Carona asked. "You know things with little buttons and a glass screen on them that fit in your hand."

"Oh, yes, we have several things that are probably what you call cell phones," Flicker replied. "The General collected the few strange devices that appeared but they don't do anything."

"Do you have any transmission towers in Boardland?" Nadie asked.

Flicker looked confused. "I'm not sure what you mean."

"Towers usually made of metal that can send electronic signals," Nadie replied.

"Nothing like that," Flicker replied.

Laughing for the first time in quite a while, Caleb exclaimed, "Then I guess those fourth graders who drew cell phones didn't realize that towers and electricity were needed for them to be of any use. Like many other people, they just use them without ever thinking of how their messages actually get to another cell phone."

Both Nadie and Carona laughed along with him but Flicker just stood looking puzzled.

"That may be funny," Nadie finally said, "but how did the General know so soon?"

"Actually," Flicker said, "some drawings have been known to train birds to carry messages."

"Like our Carrier Pigeons!" Carona added. "Not that Swoop is a pigeon, but didn't he carry a message to Flicker from us?"

"Yes, that's it!" exclaimed Caleb. "Birds in Boardland like everything else that would normally be alive in our world can talk. It makes sense that some of them might cooperate with other drawings to pass on a message to someone else! That's probably how the General's doing it. He has his spies and Fingers use certain birds!"

"You're right, although I hadn't thought much about that," Flicker added.

"I haven't seen many birds in Boardland," mentioned Carona, "but I did see one just before we left Primitivepality. It looked like a quail."

"Now I remember," Nadie added. "Just as Curly was walking away through the tall grass, I saw it fly up, remember?"

"Curly was in Primitivepality?" Flicker asked.

"Yes, he said he came because he was concerned and thought we could use his help."

"But Half Pint was already going to lead us to Impressionville so he went back," explained Nadie.

"He's sure been in places lately that he shouldn't be," Flicker replied.

"You don't think Curly could be spying for the General?" Caleb asked.

"I certainly hope not. Mr. Abe seems to trust him, but then, anything is possible. No drawing wants to be erased and Curly is certainly a candidate for that being a Scribble!" Flicker replied.

"Then maybe when we saw him across the valley with Fingers he wasn't actually captured," noted Nadie. "He might have been reporting, letting us think he was captured."

"Even if it's only a possibility we need to be careful when he's around. We'll need to apprise Mr. Abe of our concerns," cautioned Flicker. "I recommend that the three of you hurry back to the Forest of Memories. It will be dark soon."

"Yes, it will be safe there. We only have two more days before the General plans to attack Abstractshire," Caleb replied.

"Then I suggest you concentrate on your plan. There isn't much you can do about Half Pint. He knew the chances he was taking by helping you. Hopefully the General will want to keep him around," Flicker concluded.

"Then tomorrow it's off to Impressionville for us, then to Realtown," Caleb replied as Flicker disappeared.

After looking at the map Caleb discovered that there was a sky trail that passed near the Forest of Memories. Since the General was still looking for them, they decided to follow a tunnel that came up near the Forest of Memories so he wouldn't know for sure they had gotten away. Caleb thanked Groff for his help and asked if it was all right for them to use his tunnels again. Groff graciously gave them permission.

They spent several minutes running the four to five miles it took for the tunnel to come up near the main trail that entered the Forest of Memories. As they came up and moved towards the Forest they heard moaning and crying sounds. After running around a large pile of boulders they saw where the sounds were coming from.

Just where the trail entered the Forest was a pile of drawings all which were tied together. Most had been partly smudged!

"Oh no! Look what the General's Fingers have done!" Carona yelled and ran towards the pile.

Nadie and Caleb followed right behind her. As they got closer, Caleb recognized two of the drawings. Both Sketchard, from Absractshire, and Dot, from Primitivepality, were among them. Caleb, Nadie, and Carona quickly began untying them. Most were injured and scared.

"Sketchard, Dot, what happened?" Caleb asked as he untied and pulled both from the pile.

"Are we glad to see you!" Sketchard replied as he tried to stand. It was a futile attempt, since one of his legs had been smudged. "A troop of mounted Fingers attacked Abstractshire shortly after you left. They grabbed and smudged several of us as they shouted, 'troublemakers will be smudged!' and dragged us away. It was awful! They seemed to know exactly who our leaders were. We didn't even have a chance to run. At first we thought the General had come with all his troops to erase Abstractshire but they just snatched us saying they'd be back soon for the rest."

Dot, whose right arm and bonnet had been erased, lay moaning where Caleb had placed her.

"Dot, are you going to be all right?" Nadie asked.

"I think so, but being smudged hurts more than I thought it would. We couldn't believe that the

General's Fingers would attack Primitivepality. They seemed to know who our council members were. They said that any drawing rebelling against the General would be severely punished or erased."

"Caleb," Sketchard said, "as the Fingers dragged us here, they said it was a warning from the General to us and to you. They said that if we helped you and you didn't leave Boardland then you along with every city but Realtown would be destroyed!"

"How can someone who is supposed to take care of their people do such a thing?" said Carona as tears fell from her eyes.

"Power, greed, and selfishness can drive a person to do all kinds of evil things," Nadie replied, "especially when there isn't anyone to hold him accountable for his actions."

Many of the drawings, especially the scribbles, wiggled around on the ground. In some cases, it was hard to tell exactly what part of them had been smudged. Once they were separated, Carona reached into her backpack and pulled out her chalk. First, she chalked in a leg for Sketchard and then, using the white and red chalks, drew back Dot's arm and the red bonnet with white dots that had been on her head. Immediately they both felt better.

Following Carona's lead, both Caleb and Nadie started doing the same. Nadie worked on the four remaining drawings from Primitivepality since she could tell what parts had been smudged. Caleb worked on the seven other drawings from Abstractshire as Sketchard identified for him what needed to be drawn to replace the parts that had been smudged.

The drawings couldn't believe how the Talbots could draw them back together and continued to thank them as they drew.

"Fortunately, none of us were smudged, and erased or we'd be gone forever," Dot said as she tried to help her friends.

"The General had set a trap for us in Rockbound Valley. We were lucky to get away," Caleb shared. "Looks like the General knows what we're up to and is not only trying to destroy us but to intimidate any drawing in Boardland who may be helping us. He's very devious, attacking in two places at once!"

"I'm not about to be intimidated by anyone," Sketchard yelled out, "especially since his plans may be to erase all but Realtown! I'd rather be erased fighting than to be erased some night when I slept!"

"That goes for me too," Dot added. "Now we know what his long-term plans really are! We have a rallying point for the drawings from at least three of Boardland's cities!"

"We're glad to see this terrible event hasn't dampened your desire for freedom," Nadie noted. "But it looks like there may be more sacrifices to come."

"At least we have the Talbots to help us in a fight. If we're erased they can draw us back to our artist's original rendition," Sketchard added. "We want to thank you again. We should get our friends back to town and let everyone know what happened. Call us when you need us!"

As Sketchard, Dot, and their friends hurried back home, the Talbots headed towards their house in the Forest of Memories. The Illuminator's light was almost out, leaving a strange brownish-white glow on the horizon. They had not seen such a glow the night before. Caleb figured it must have been caused by the remainder of the General's chalk storm settling low in the sky.

Chapter Nine

No Escape, But Chalk Power

"I don't like all this," Nadie said as they entered the house, tossing their backpacks into the hall closet. "It keeps getting more complicated."

"I feel that way too," replied Caleb.

"For the first time I'm a little scared," Carona shared. "At first, I felt that since we were doing the right thing in helping the drawings and were real people, we could be captured but not really hurt. Now I'm not only concerned about the drawings in Boardland but about our welfare too."

"Yes, I know the feeling, but we're trapped. We gave our word and we, the Legend, are the only hope these drawings have," Caleb replied. "I for one think we need to be sure we can leave when we want. If we know we can always escape we'd be more likely to do all that it takes to win…except maybe totally sacrifice ourselves."

"But Caleb, isn't that what it takes sometimes, to be willing to totally sacrifice yourself for what you believe?" Nadie asked.

"That's probably the meaning of a true hero, the ultimate courageous act of sacrifice and love," Caleb replied. "Yet we have to remember that we're talking about sacrificing ourselves for a world we're not a part of, for a world which in many ways is a fantasy existing of chalk drawings behind a blackboard, a world as mostly fourth graders envision it. How much sacrificing do we do for such a place? It's not like our own world, family, or friends. There has to be a difference there somewhere."

"Well, I know we've made a commitment," said Nadie. "Just how far I'm willing to go I'm still not sure. I do agree that we should see if there is a way out of Boardland for when we want or need to leave. After all, as you remember we were told that we could return by both Flicker and Mr. Abe. It's just that "when the time is right" thing for leaving was added after we said we'd enter. That changed everything. In a way, we were tricked! That was an important change. Had I known that we couldn't leave until someone else or thing decided we could, I never would have crawled into that tunnel."

"I think we should find a way out too," Carona shared. "Even though I'm afraid, after we knew about the change we still agreed to help. I say we look for a way out but keep in mind that we still made a commitment."

"Then first thing in the morning we travel back to the indigo mountain and find the cave that takes us out through the blackboard. After that we go to Impressionville and then to Realtown to have a long talk with Mr. Abe. We all have a lot of questions to ask before we finalize any plan."

As soon as the Illuminator's light came on, Nadie and Carona dashed down the stairs to the kitchen only to find that Caleb was already there. He'd been drawing on the white wall behind the kitchen table with his chalk.

"What are you doing?" Nadie asked as they entered.

"Just seeing what this chalk actually does."

"And?" Nadie asked.

"As you can see I can draw things on the wall's surfaces that magically become real objects, like the picture and frame I've laid on the table. I drew them on the wall and when I finished I could actually take them off and lay them down. The people in the picture just stay on the surface. I can't make drawings that come alive. Looks like we can draw inanimate things but nothing that comes to life! I guess those things have to come through the blackboard. We know we can replace things that have been smudged by drawing back what the original artist intended. However, we can't change features on a live drawing."

Nadie who had been carefully listening asked, "Then if we have to fight the General and his Fingers, any drawing that they smudge we can quickly repair, right?"

"Yeah, I guess so, as long as they're not completely erased. If that happens, then I don't think we can redraw them."

"That power will really help us when the smudging and erasing starts, but we'll have to act fast. Knowing that should make the drawings feel better about helping us," Nadie noted.

"Caleb," said Carona, "can you draw a picture of a blackboard eraser?"

"I think so," he replied and he pulled out a piece of blue chalk and drew a blue blackboard eraser on the wall. Then he covered it over with yellow and red chalk.

"Why are you doing that?" Carona asked.

"Because," replied Caleb, "that's what you have to use if you have the colors of the rainbow and want to make black...see," he said as his blue eraser slowly turned grayish black.

"Where did you learn that?" Nadie asked.

"Just the other day I had a teacher who told us about the color wheel they use in art. When you only have certain colors, you can mix them to make all kinds of other colors. Pretty neat, Huh?"

"Yeah, but can you take it off the wall?" Carona asked.

"Yep," Caleb said as he reached up and took it magically in his hand. "Just like the framed picture I drew."

"But how does it feel? Can it erase chalk?" Carona continued to ask.

Caleb made several small circles on the wall using various colors of chalk then pushed the eraser across them. Immediately the chalk lines disappeared.

"Looks like they can," he replied as Carona began to smile.

It only took Caleb a moment to realize what Carona had just learned.

"Weapons!" he said.

"Now I see," exclaimed Nadie, "We can draw a hundred of these then give them to the drawings to use against the General and his Fingers! He'd never expect it. We could overpower them. With so many of us erasing and so few of them, the odds are we would win, especially if we could quickly re-chalk those drawings that were only partly smudged or erased. Maybe we do have a chance!"

Nadie and Carona brought their chalk to the kitchen where they all spent a few minutes drawing various objects. Then they gleefully lifted them from the wall and laid them on the table. Carona was especially excited when she drew a banana, then lifted it from the wall and ate it for breakfast! Not being the best artist, Caleb drew what looked like a large cinnamon roll. Nadie bet him he wouldn't eat that 'weird thing', but he did licking his partially chalked fingers as he swallowed the last piece.

"This is a lot of fun but we have much to do today," Caleb said. "First we need to check out the indigo mountain and find the way out of Boardland. Then we need to do a quick run to Impressionville to gain their support, and follow it up with a trip to Realtown and a talk with Mr. Abe."

By the time Caleb had reminded them of what they needed to do, both of his sisters had pulled their backpacks from the closet and were heading out the front door. As they came down the stairs, Spring suddenly bounced up.

"Hi," she giggled. "I couldn't wait for you to come out. It is really sad what the General did yesterday. It just makes more of us realize how glad we are that the Talbots are here to help us!"

Caleb was momentarily caught off guard by Spring's appearance. He had forgotten that she said she'd stay around to help them. Now, when they were going to look for a possible escape route from Boardland, was not a good time to have her with them.

"Oh, Spring," Caleb said, "we're so glad to see you...because we... have an errand for you."

Spring began to bounce with excitement. "Yes, yes, what do you want me to do?"

"We need you to go on ahead of us to Impressionville and tell the village leaders that we will be there mid-morning to talk with them. That won't be too dangerous for you will it?" Caleb asked.

Spring stopped bouncing and seemed to be processing the question. "No, Caleb, I don't think so. I will have to be extra careful just as you will have to be with the General and his Fingers lurking behind every tree. I'm not supposed to go there but I do have a friend or two in Impressionville who I'm sure will help us."

"Good! Then we'll see you in a little while. Thank you for your help," Caleb called after Spring as she turned around and was bouncing away.

"Good job, Caleb," said Nadie. "Having Spring with us would have complicated things."

Caleb glanced at the map and started jogging then running along the trail leading out of the Forest of Memories. After leaving the Forest, Caleb led them through the brush and trees just to the right of the road in case a trap had been set or a spy was watching. Soon they approached Carona's meadow and ran towards the indigo mountain and the rocks just below.

"This is where we came out when we arrived with Flicker two days ago," said Carona.

"It seems like we've been in Boardland for a week already," Nadie replied.

Scrutinizing every inch of the mountainside in front of them, Caleb said, "I know there were a few bushes in front of the opening but I don't even see them now."

Nadie and Carona walked along the base of the mountain looking for any signs of an opening. Suddenly Nadie stopped and stared down at her feet.

"Why'd you stop, Nadie?" Carona asked.

Nadie just pointed down. Caleb had joined them.

"Hey!" said Carona. "Those are our footprints on the ground. They're coming right out of the side of the mountain, except there's no cave, just solid rock."

Caleb picked up a rock and began hitting the mountainside just above the footprints.

"Wow, it feels solid to me. We must be doing something wrong. The cave and tunnel have to be inside." Caleb couldn't believe that they might be stuck in Boardland forever.

"We have to find a way out of Boardland!" Nadie exclaimed as she pushed on the mountainside.

"Wait a minute," Carona shouted as she reached into her backpack and pulled out her indigo chalk. "After I drew the mountain remember how you told me to draw a cave, Caleb?"

"Yes, a cave, and then I held you up while you drew a rainbow above it!"

Carona reached as high as she could and arched a thick indigo chalk mark above the footprints then brought it down both sides to the ground. "Now, Caleb, hold me up so I can do the rainbow."

"I'll hand you each of the seven colors, Carona," said Nadie as Caleb lifted her.

A moment later the arched opening had a rainbow of colors above it. The three of them stood back and waited.

"Nothing's happening," Nadie said as she touched the mountainside.

Pounding with a rock where the opening should have been Caleb shouted, "We must be doing something wrong!"

"Of course, you are," a voice sang out making them all jump. They all turned at once to see Flicker behind them.

"Flicker, what are you doing here?" Caleb asked.

"The Illuminator told me to be here this morning. I could only have guessed why."

Nadie, feeling like she'd been caught with her hand in the cookie jar replied. "We were just...ah...seeing if the cave was still here."

Flicker smiled and said, "Don't you remember that it will only be there under the rainbow when the time is right?"

"Yes, yes, we remember, but we don't like feeling that we can't leave when we want to. It's not that we plan to leave just yet. We only wanted to know we could," Caleb replied.

"I think I understand," said Flicker.

"Besides," Caleb continued, "when we first saw you, we were told we'd be coming just for a visit and could go back if we wanted to!"

"Yes, but you seem to forget that I also said 'when all things come together', and they haven't yet."

"Then we can't leave now even if we wanted?" Carona asked.

"I wish it were that easy, but before you leave one way or the other, the Legend has to be fulfilled. That will be when the time is right."

"But what about the rainbow and our chalk?" Nadie asked.

"As you know the chalk you each have allows you to do some very magical things, all which will help you succeed. As for the rainbow, you'll need the same kind of rainbow that brought all the drawings here, to open your way home."

"But I just drew a rainbow on the mountainside, Flicker," said Carona.

"Yes, I see. That was a part of it, but you're missing the rainbow that allowed all the drawings to come through the blackboard in the first place," Flicker replied.

Caleb looking a bit confused.

"But Flicker, we did everything we did before."

"Besides the time not being right, you need the rainbow," he replied.

"Okay, then what and where is it?" asked Caleb.

"I'm afraid that has to be part of your plan for saving Boardland and going home. You must figure that out for yourselves. So far, you've discovered most of the gifts you'll need for your plan to work. You have all done very well. I and the Great Illuminator are very pleased with you."

"But Flicker…" Nadie began to say when suddenly he was gone.

"Why can't people just tell us what we need to do? It would be so much easier," said Nadie.

Frowning, Carona said, "I suppose that's part of the Legend too. Heroes don't just do what they're told. They figure it out for themselves, take risks, and then have the courage to act."

Caleb looked at Carona. "Are you sure you're my little sister? You always seem to have the insight of an adult."

Carona blushed as Caleb rubbed the top of her head.

"Well, that was disappointing," Caleb added. "I hope we can figure out what Flicker was talking about or we may be living in the Forest of Memories and Nadie's house for a long time. That is something we talked about doing a few days ago, living in a house like Nadie's. I don't think we ever meant to do it here. We'd better head towards Impressionville for our meeting with the town leaders. I told Spring to tell them we'd be there mid-morning."

"I say we throw caution to the wind and use a sky trail. We might as well be enjoying our powers since we may be using them for the rest of our lives," Nadie suggested.

"I'd like that. Let's fly!" Carona added.

Caleb had already pulled the map out and found a sky trail that would take them near Impressionville.

"Sounds good! Follow me!" he shouted as he started running, preparing for his jump.

As the three of them jumped, the words 'high in the sky' echoed off the face of the mountain and across the meadow. They quickly gained elevation. Caleb flew as high as he felt comfortable with the hope of not being spotted from below. Shortly, Impressionville came into view. Caleb wondered what would happen if they just kept right on flying. Did Boardland end just over the horizon? If not, what could possibly be beyond it, another blackboard world? Or could they fly out into the real world? Caleb felt it was strange that he hadn't considered those possibilities before.

They landed in a forest opening a few hundred yards from the village. Right away they could see the difference between the trees and plants near Impressionville and Abstractshire. In Abstractshire everything seemed disjointed and strange with most structures and even drawings of people distorted or misshapen. It was often difficult to understand what the artist actually had in mind. Now the three siblings could see what each drawing represented even though they often seemed fuzzy or blurry, like they'd been blown in the wind. The branches and bows of some trees looked like they were drawn by dabbing or even a bit of smudging! As they approached the village the houses and cottages looked bright but slightly blurred. Even the flowers with their brilliant colors were identifiable but unfocused.

"I like this kind of drawing even when the artist uses colored chalk," Carona shared,

"There's a sense of peacefulness to it like I'm almost in a dream world."

"This is the drawing style used by artists like Renoir and Monet. I heard about them from our teacher. They use short, broken brush strokes, and light, bright and varied colors. It's very pleasing. You can always tell what the artist was meaning to draw. I can sort of see some fourth graders drawing some of this artwork but others must have been drawn by Ms. Colton or Mrs. Durham," Nadie stated.

Caleb surveyed the landscape. "When I was in room 7, we used to have an art teacher come and teach us on Tuesday afternoons. She used to do some artwork in this style. Maybe she partly built Impressionville."

"Hey, look!" Carona said as she pointed at a sentence whose letters had legs and was running down the street. The three of them watched as it ran by, yelling out, 'There's no place like home, there's no place like home!"

"They'd better be running", Caleb said. "They need to get back to Abstractshire soon or they'll be erased!"

"Carona, has Mrs. Durham read The Wizard of Oz to your class yet?" Nadie asked.

"Yes, we actually just finished that part where Dorothy clicks her ruby shoes together and says 'There's no place like home', in order to go back to Kansas."

Nadie, paused for a moment. "I wish it were that easy for us. This rainbow and the 'time is right' thing have us trapped. I think we should still try to help, but I don't like feeling controlled."

Looking up the street they saw Spring bounding towards them. Running along next to her was a young girl with long yellow-blond hair wearing a yellow sundress. Her hair was waving behind her and it almost matched the yellow in her dress.

"The Talbots are here!" they could hear Spring yelling as she bounded up to them.

"Hi! Everyone is waiting for you in the town hall. Zephyr, the Mayor, is there along with most of the drawings that can move. They are all very excited."

"Thanks Spring, for helping us. We'll follow you to the hall," replied Caleb with a smile.

Spring blushed then said, "Oh, yes, I almost forgot. This is my friend, Puff. She's lived in

Impressionville for many years. We don't get to see each other very often, but we sneak a visit every once in a while. She looks young, but she's also on the city council and knows everything that goes on here and in Boardland."

"It's nice to meet you," Caleb said, "and these are my sisters, Nadie and Carona," he added as Puff took each of their hands and shook them.

"That's the first time I've ever shaken hands with someone who didn't return chalk to mine, real people. I never thought the Legend would actually come true. We all had hoped, but since the General was getting more and more powerful, it seemed less possible every year. I can't believe the day has finally come."

"Thank you for waiting for us, Puff," Nadie said. "We're glad we can help."

Carona looked at Spring and said, "I'm afraid you may be seen here by a spy and get smudged."

"So am I, a little, but Puff has a secret place for me to hide where I'll be safe in case the Fingers come after me."

"A secret place?" Carona replied.

"Oh yes. Most drawings in Boardland have places they can hide, especially the Scribbles and Scrawls like me. We never know when the General may pass a new regulation regarding drawings or want to punish someone. A few times his Fingers have found a drawing's hiding place. Usually, once we're safely hidden, they won't find us."

"That's good to know," a relieved Carona replied.

Spring turned and bounded up the street with Puff running next to her. They moved left at the first corner and headed down a tree lined street that led to a beautiful tall building. The building sat on one side of a large rectangular park obviously drawn and used as a town center. Even a sizable white ornamented pavilion sat in the park.

All three Talbots stopped for a moment awestruck by the grandeur of the town hall building.

"That looks like the picture of the gothic cathedral in France I was just looking at in my world history class," Caleb mentioned. "I'd like to meet the artist who drew that on the blackboard!"

As they entered through the decorative wooden doors the Talbots were surprised to see a huge bright, open room, filled with most of the inhabitants of Impressionville. Luminous colored lights streamed in from several large stained-glass windows. Seeing the enormity and beauty of the room, Carona wanted to jump up and fly throughout the building and explore the many stories the windows must have portrayed. Her mind was quickly brought back to the drawings that were cheering and yelling their names.

Then a tall, slim man, wearing a blue sports coat and light blue jeans, came forward with his hand outstretched. Behind him was a lady with an alluring smile whose face seemed to sparkle. She was wearing a flowing evening gown striped with many brilliant colors. Everyone fell silent as the man began to speak.

"Welcome, welcome to Impressionville. We've heard so much about you over the last couple of days and are overjoyed to finally meet the legendary Talbots!" he said. "I'm Zephyr, the Mayor."

Shaking his hand, Caleb replied. "And we're glad to finally visit you."

"Yes, and I'm pleased to introduce you to Prism, who's been a Council member for as long as anyone can remember."

Prism stepped forward and leisurely shook their hands while clearly studying each of their faces.

"It's been so long that the Legend has kept our hope alive for freedom, the kind of freedom we had before the General's despotic rule. Now, with your help, maybe all drawings can be respected again for whom and what they are."

Instantly the Talbots were captivated by Prism's voice and presence. It was hard to remain focused on her since she shown nearly as bright as the stained-glass windows.

"Spring, for one, has told us about you," Zephyr shared. "We know you've been to Abstractshire and Primitivepality and gained their support in your quest against the General."

Quickly, Caleb spoke up. "Actually, Mr. Mayor, not to be disrespectful, it's your quest, with our help.

We understand the Legend and have discovered the reasons you and the citizens of Boardland can't get rid of the General and his Fingers by yourselves. We can't break his rule without your help."

"Yes, yes," Zephyr quickly replied. "The council and our citizens understand that. Our problem has been convincing everyone that we should fight with you to destroy his rule. Many of us feel that life hasn't been all that bad since he took over. Few of us have been smudged or erased, and when that has happened it's because some of us have broken a law or fought against him. Otherwise he leaves Impressionville drawings alone because of our artistic merit!"

"Now you must understand that the General plans to erase not just Abstractshire, but everyone else except Realtown," Nadie shared.

"We have heard that rumor," Zephyr replied.

"It's not a rumor!" Nadie immediately exclaimed. "Just late yesterday near the Forest of Memories, we came across a group of partly smudged and erased leaders from Abstractshire and Primitivepality. Sketchard, from Abstractshire, was told by the Fingers that if anyone helped us they would be erased as would every city but Realtown."

A loud gasp came from the room and echoed throughout the hall.

"So, no city or drawing from anywhere but Realtown is safe," Nadie concluded.

"I understand what you're saying, but I find it hard to believe," replied the Mayor.

Immediately Prism spoke up. "Mr. Mayor, you have the information coming directly from Nadie Talbot, of our great Legend. She is a real person with nothing to gain by lying. You would put the possibility of us not overthrowing the evil rule of the General and fulfilling the Legend because you choose to question its validity? How absurd! The Council has had many discussions on his matter over the years. Most of us realize that we must fight. Do you intend to support the General's rule for eternity?"

Immediately there were shouts from the masses. "Destroy the General! Long live the Legend! The time is right! Prism is right. Long live the Talbots!"

As more and more drawings began to shout, Spring couldn't restrain herself. She began to bounce around the hall singing, "Finally we'll be free The Eraser is going to flee. The Fingers will follow. We'll be merry tomorrow, and all live happily!" She continued to bounce and sing the verses over and over again until a choir of voices filled the Hall.

The Mayor stood with a sheepish grin on his face. "My apologies," he said as he bowed towards Nadie. I'm afraid it's hard for me to believe anything I hear these days. Thank you, Prism, for pointing out one of my many faults, and thank you everyone for voting with your song! Caleb, Nadie, Carona, we'll be pleased to do anything required to help you rid

Boardland of the General. By saying this, and knowing that there are probably spies present, I put myself and everyone here in danger. However, the price of freedom has never come without sacrifice, whatever that may be!"

Once more the citizens began chanting and singing Spring's song as she gleefully joined in. The whole hall seemed to sway as the drawings' voices and the light beams from the stained-glass windows undulated together.

"Then you'll be ready when we need you?" Caleb asked.

Mayor Zephyr raised his hands shouting, "We will!" and a tumultuous echo of voices followed with, "We will! We will!"

Realizing it was almost noon and they had hoped to get to Realtown and spend some time with Mr. Abe, Caleb thanked the Mayor, Prism and the drawings of Impressionville for their support. As he said goodbye, Carona tapped him on the shoulder and whispered, "Caleb, don't you think we should begin to arm our friends with erasers with which to fight? We may need their help at any time. If we don't, how are we going to get them to all of the towns?" Caleb paused then whispered back to Carona and Nadie.

"Mr. Mayor, is there someplace we could talk privately?" Caleb asked.

Zephyr, replied, "Of course, there is a room just off to the right which I use as my office. Please follow me."

The Talbots, along with Prism and Spring, followed the Mayor to his office. It was a comfortable office with a single window looking out towards the village. The furnishings in no way matched the style or elegance of the building. There was a small bookcase, a simple oak desk and several tall back leather chairs scattered around the rather plain room.

"Mr. Mayor . . . ," Caleb began.

"Please call me Zephyr," the Mayor interrupted, "I only use my title with the public to sound important. The citizens seem to like it."

"Of course, Zephyr. We need to leave some things with you that the General does not allow you to have. We don't want anyone to know what they are until we call upon you for your help. We'd like to fill three bags with what we consider to be tools you can use against the General and his Fingers. After we leave we'd like you to send one of the three bags to Coal in Primitivepality, and the other to Sketchard in Abstractshire. They should be told to tell no one about the bags until the time is right. When that happens, you'll know what to do."

Zephyr looking confused.

"I'm not sure what you have in mind or what you're planning to leave behind. However, I realize it is important to our goal so I'll gladly do as you ask."

"Thank you for trusting us. But may we ask another favor? We need to use your office for a while to assemble the bags...that is, if you don't mind," Caleb continued.

"Oh, okay, fine. We'll all leave until you call for us," a hesitating Zephyr replied as he left the room along with Prism and Spring.

"We need to work quickly and quietly," said Caleb. "Take the chalk from your backpacks and put your backpacks in that closet like we do at home. We're going to need all the room we can get."

Then Caleb told them that Carona was right. They needed to get the erasers to everyone as soon as they could, but because of spies, they shouldn't trust anyone. Even the unfamiliar walls in the room might have ears. He quietly told them to draw as many blackboard erasers of any color and of various sizes they chose. Then as fast as they could they should take their drawings off the wall and fill each of the three large bags he would draw. Immediately the three of them began drawing erasers on the walls of the office.

An hour and a half later, the Talbots had filled and tied three large gunny sack bags with one hundred and fifty erasers each. Zephyr said he'd be sure to protect them and secretly send a bag each on to Coal and Sketchard. Spring said she would show them the quickest way to Realtown as long as they planned to stay on the ground. The three of them immediately set off for Realtown to visit Mr. Abe with Spring leading the way. They hoped to get some questions answered and size up the amount of resistance they would get from the drawings living there.

Chapter Ten

Trapped and Other Surprises

"Are all my men in position?" the General asked the Captain.

"Yes, my General. They are covering every road and trail from Impressionville to Realtown. Are you sure they are coming this way?"

"Positive! They'll be here in just a few minutes!" the General replied trying not to smile.

"In just a few minutes?" the Captain asked. "Our spies have not yet reported their current location." Captain Thumb, noticing the General's huge grin, wondered why the General seemed so amused.

"I really don't need information from our spies for I have known most of what the Talbots have been doing for some time. I have my own way."

"My General, then you are sure they are coming by land? If they are coming by air we must move closer to town and surround any open spaces."

"By land! Now you do have the nets, ropes and cavalrymen hidden in the trees, don't you? No open spaces where they can jump into the sky. We must take them completely by surprise."

"Of course, just as you instructed!"

"Soon, with the Talbots along with their Legend locked in my dungeon, no one from Boardland will ever think of questioning my authority or my artistic integrity again! This time they will not get away!"

Caleb knew that having Spring bounding alone in front slowed them down. But she had helped so much he was glad she found such joy in leading them to Realtown. He decided to run along next to her for a few miles.

"We really appreciate your help, Spring, and especially you getting the drawings in Impressionville ready for us."

Spring was thrilled by what Caleb said. "Thank you, Caleb, for letting me assist you in making the Legend come true. Just imagine, a Scribble helping the Talbots get rid of the General!"

"It takes a lot of courage and you have loads of that," Caleb replied. "I hope we find Mr. Abe at home. We have many questions for him, questions about Boardland's earliest history and how our names became part of the Legend."

"Oh, you could have asked Rainbow about that!"

"Who's Rainbow?" Caleb asked.

"I'm sorry, few call her Rainbow anymore. I meant, Prism."

"Prism was called Rainbow?"

"That was sort of her nickname because when the sun light shines on her just right she reflects a beautiful rainbow, that's why."

Caleb, thinking for a moment about Prism's nickname asked, "How could she have answered our questions?"

"She was one of the first drawings to enter Boardland about the same time as Mr. Abe, that's why," replied Spring.

Caleb couldn't believe it. Maybe he had found the rainbow that would open the tunnel and let them leave Boardland. Their chalk couldn't do it, but a rainbow from a prism like the one hanging in Room 7 might be the key. As he continued to analyze the situation he realized the prism's rainbow reflection against the blackboard could be one of the reasons there was a Boardland. It could even be the bright light that brought Flicker through the board to speak to them. Wow, he thought. Prism would know as much about Boardland as Mr. Abe, maybe even more. He couldn't help but smile as he continued along the wooded trail. Now he was even more anxious to talk to Mr. Abe.

"Can you bounce any faster, Spring?" an excited Caleb shouted.

She turned smiling, "Of course," came the reply and immediately sped up.

At that moment Caleb saw a shadow moving above him and felt something hard hit his head and slide off his back. A scream rang out as he recognized Nadie's voice. Fingers appeared around them. "A trap!" he yelled. Knowing they couldn't jump and fly in such a wooded area he yelled again, "Keep running as fast as you can!" but it was too late. As he looked behind them he could see Nadie and Carona squirming under a large net. If he and Spring hadn't just sped up, they would be in it too. He knew there was nothing he could do. If he stopped running to help he would be captured like his sisters. Besides, he and Spring had several cavalrymen with ropes galloping just behind them.

Spring yelled, "Follow me!" She quickly bounded into the thickest part of the forest.

Two Fingers were knocked off their horses by low hanging branches as another horseman tried to ride between two trees causing his horse to tumble. A moment later the cavalrymen stopped their chase.

"What do we do now?" Spring asked.

Still not believing they'd been caught in a trap and that his sisters were probably on their way to the General's dungeon, Caleb replied, "It won't do us any good to go after them. They'll expect that. Besides I don't think the General will hurt them. He'll probably use them as bait to draw me in. I need to talk to Mr.

Abe and put our final plan in motion as soon as possible. I'll find the closest tunnel to his house. We can't be seen. I'm sure the General's Fingers will be everywhere in Realtown looking for me."

Within a minute Caleb had identified a tunnel opening on his map near the forest they'd run into. From there he found another tunnel which came up a few houses from Mr. Abe's. Without delay they both made their way into the tunnel.

Carona had stopped crying as several Fingers loosened the net and pushed them into the back of an old truck with a homemade camper shell on its bed.

Both Nadie and Carona were still shaken by the surprise trap and the realization that they were now under the control of the ruthless General. They hoped that Caleb and Spring had escaped. As they peered out the small back window, they saw the General ride up, stop behind the truck, and with a bizarre smile wave at them as the truck lunged forward.

"What are we going to do, Nadie?"

"The only thing we can do, Carona. Look for a chance to escape when they take us to the General's dungeon."

Carona frowned and shook her head. "I sure hope they don't torture us. I don't think I'd be very good at that."

"Don't worry I'm sure their attention is now aimed at finding Caleb. They know that without him we're still a threat and the Legend lives on."

Sure enough, they found themselves being led down some stairs into the musky and dusty dungeon under the Castle.

"Am I sorry to see the two of you here," they heard a voice say from a cell next to the one they were pushed into.

Through the dim light they were able to make out Half Pint.

"We are too, Half Pint," Nadie replied, "but Caleb's still free and I'm sure he'll have a plan to rescue us very soon. It's good to see they haven't smudged or erased you."

"I'm really not sure why they haven't. I guess it's because they've been so busy trying to trap you."

"And how is Curly?" Carona asked.

A disgusted look appeared on Half Pint's face as he curled his lip under. "Curly told on us. He is one of the General's main spies. The General probably knows all about you by now since Curly was with you so much."

"We were afraid of that. We think he's been using quail to send messages. When we saw him with you and the Fingers in Rockbound Valley we thought something was fishy," Nadie explained. "He seemed so nice. What would ever make a drawing turn on his own kind?"

"It didn't take me long to figure that out," Half Pint replied. "Look down a-ways to the last large cell. See all the letters and numbers locked in it?"

Nadie pushed her head up against the cell's bars and looked.

"Yes, when we snuck into the castle a couple of days ago during Recess, we opened their cell and let them out, but it looks like the General caught most of them."

"Well," said Half Pint, "in that cell are the letters R and S. They are actually drawings who have arms, and legs and like Curly Q are animated. Curly considers, R his wife, and S, his daughter. I figure he didn't have much of a choice but to be a spy. I'm sure the General threatened to erase them if he didn't help. He knows that very few drawings that enter the dungeon are ever seen again."

"Not to say Curly did the right thing, but it must be hard on him to turn on his friends like that," shared Carona.

"Yes," replied Half Pint, "but our very existence depends upon the Legend being fulfilled."

Sure enough, the tunnel Caleb and Spring had taken came up in the shrub filled back yard of a sizable A-frame on Lovely Lane. The house was just three backyards away from Mr. Abe's American Colonial home in the cul-de-sac. Caleb and Spring had no problem jumping the fences between the yards ending up at Mr. Abe's sturdy white back door.

They quietly circled the house looking in the windows as well as into the cul-de-sac for any indication of lurking Fingers. Seeing none they returned to the back door and knocked. After a short time, they saw Mary peeking out a side window. Soon the door opened.

"Sorry we have to sneak up on you, Mrs. Abe," said Caleb. "It's of vital importance that we speak to Mr. Abe."

Mary looked at them for a moment then nodded her head. "Mr. Abe has been expecting you. You'll find him in the living room."

As they entered the room Mr. Abe put a book down, stood, and with a warm smile greeted them.

"Caleb, I'm so glad you're here. And Spring it's good to see you again. Where are Nadie and Carona?"

"The General discovered that we were traveling by land to Realtown and set a trap for us. His net caught them. Spring and I were lucky to get away. I imagine he has taken them to his castle."

Abe's smile changed to a wrinkled frown. "I'm very sorry to hear that. I know you're already thinking of a way to rescue them."

"At this point the rescue many include most of Broadland,"

"Then please have a seat. I know you have questions although I'm sure in your travels you've discovered the answers to many of them."

"Yes, now we have a useful understanding of what Boardland is all about as well as the severity of its problems," Caleb replied.

"Do you mind if I ask a few questions first?" Abe asked. Caleb nodded.

"First, have you discovered anymore special gifts?"

"The map you provided has been very useful. We met Groff and learned that many of the lines on the map indicated tunnels which we have often used with Groff's consent. We discovered that in Boardland we can see not only in the dark tunnels but at night as well. Also, apparently due to our real nature, we can run faster than the General's best horsemen and jump as high as a medium sized tree. This has allowed us to travel around Boardland in a very short period of time."

"All these have served you well," Mr. Abe replied.

Caleb looked puzzled, "But Mr. Abe, you must know about these gifts as well as our ability to fly within restricted sky trails."

"You can fly too?" Abe asked.

"Of course, we discovered that gift while trying to figure out what the trail lines in the sky meant on your map."

"Oh, I see. You assumed that since I sent you the map I drew the map?"

"You didn't draw the map?"

"No, it was given to me years ago by Gleam. I was merely it's guardian until the time was right and the Talbots arrived."

"Then who drew the map and why didn't Gleam give it to us?" Caleb asked.

"I assumed it was created by the Great Illuminator shortly after the General took power and the Legend became known," Mr. Abe replied. "It was his gift to help us rid Boardland of the General and his evil rule."

"Why doesn't the Great Illuminator just rid Boardland of the General himself?"

"No one knows for sure, but I think it has something to do with him giving us light and animation as drawings so we can solve our own problems. When he realized how difficult it was for us to challenge the giant Eraser, the map appeared and so did the start of the Legend. We were given one more chance and that chance was the Talbots!"

"How did he know someday we'd arrive in Boardland and even know our names?" Caleb asked.

"That I do not know. All I can say is the Great Illuminator and his light were the first to come through the Blackboard. As I understand it, in many ways he rules in your real world as he does in ours. Maybe he knew about you from your world."

"Did you and Prism come through with him?"

"Oh, so you met Prism. No, we came shortly after. We were the first drawings to come through since we were the first drawn on the board. Actually, Prism was drawn or etched by her creator's bright rainbow colors reflected on the board. I think her creator was a prism hanging in Room 7, not Mrs. Colton, who was my Creator."

"Wow, this is all so amazing," Caleb exclaimed

"Did you discover anything else that might help you with your plan?"

"We found that the citizens of Abstractshire, Primitivepality and Impressionville along with their leaders will help us."

"All three cities will help?"

"Yes, their leaders, Sketchard, Coal, and Zephy.r pledged their loyalty... and we have the support of Gleam, Flicker, Spark, and a reluctant Swoop! I'd say our army has grown since we arrived!" Caleb proudly added. "Oh, I almost forgot, we also managed to take the General's look a-like stuffed doll from him when he was asleep during Recess. You never know when his favorite sleep toy may come in handy."

"You took the General's stuffed likeness?" Mr. Abe asked.

"Yes, I've kept it with me in my backpack except when I'm resting. Then I put my backpack in the closet. You seemed surprised."

"I am! There are two problems with you having it. First, the General seldom naps during Recess. He seems to be immune from it. He only rests since no one else can assist him at that time. Secondly, hearsay has it that a small likeness of him does exist which was drawn at the same time he was and came through the blackboard with him. It is also said that the likeness is as animated and active as he is! Where is it now?" Mr. Abe asked.

"I always keep it closed in my backpack which I'm usually wearing. Would you like to see it?"

"No, thank you, but I would like your backpack if you'd please hand it to me."

Caleb was still processing the idea that the stuffed likeness of General that he'd carried on his back for two days may be alive, or at least animated. He immediately handed his backpack to Mr. Abe who took it to a far closet, tossed it in, and closed the door.

"Why did you do that?" Caleb asked.

"Did you ever feel like General Eraser seemed to know where you were going and what you were up to at about the same time you did?" Mr. Abe asked.

"It did seem that way, but we knew spies like Curley, who always seemed to be hanging around us, were sending quail, like carrier pigeons, to give him information about us."

"Curley was sending information about you to the General?"

"Yes, we believe he even helped the General trap us in Rockbound Valley and capture Half Pint."

Curley, are you sure?"

"As we were trying to fly away we saw him with a group of Fingers."

Mr. Abe was obviously troubled. "I trusted him! He always used to keep me informed about the General and his Fingers' movement around Boardland."

"Perhaps that's why he knew so much," Caleb replied.

"It's possible you're right. However, it's also possible that most of the General's information came from you and your sisters."

"What? What do you mean?" replied a confused Caleb.

"If the stories are right about the General's small likeness, and he was listening to the three of you from your backpack all this time, he could have been telling the General!"

"I can't believe that!" Caleb exclaimed. "How?"

"The story says that they have a symbiotic relationship. That's like having a twin who knows and thinks exactly what you know and think. So, anything one hears the other one does too."

"That's hard to believe."

"Maybe hard to believe in the real world but remember, you're in Boardland and you just told me you can fly. I've not seen you fly, but I believe you. Strange things happen here," replied Mr. Abe.

"I get your point," Caleb said. "So the Little General may be alive in my backpack in the closet? He felt like a stuffed toy when I grabbed him and put him in my backpack. He also felt chalky."

Mr. Abe smiled, "Of course he would. He and the General may have tricked you. Neither was probably asleep. He'd likely heard from one of his spies you were coming."

"Maybe even Curley since he was in your house that night."

"That's true," Mr. Abe replied.

"Let's see what this thing is made of," Caleb said as he moved to the closet. He took his backpack in hand and laid it on the floor. "Let me try something before I open it."

Caleb felt his pack to see where the Little General was and brought his hand down hard on it. "Hey, watch it! Oops!"

"Did you hear that?" Caleb said.

"I certainly did!" replied a surprised Mr. Abe. "Looks like the stories were right!"

Caleb hit his bag again. "Okay! Okay! So, what do you want?"

"I want to know if you've been telling the General about our movement and plans," Caleb asked.

"What do you think? Do you think I wanted to ride around on your sweaty back for two days for no reason? Of course, he knows. He even knows about this conversation. Why do you think we've been able to rule Boardland for so long without having a few tricks up our sleeves? And when are you going to let me out of this smelly thing? Half my chalk has rubbed off!"

"Now since I control your world, I'm not letting you out. I like it where you are. Maybe I'll use you as my teddy," Caleb replied trying to annoy the Little General enough so he'd share more information.

"You can't treat me that way!"

"Maybe I'll just treat you like you treat the drawings…I'll just smudge, then erase you into oblivion!"

"You wouldn't dare!"

With that Caleb pounded his backpack for a third time.

"Hey, stop that," yelled the voice from the pack. "Maybe you would erase me. However, it seems we're at a standoff."

Caleb couldn't figure out what he meant. "A standoff?"

"Sure, you have me, who the General wants back, but he has your sisters, Nadie and Carona, whom I can only assume you want back."

Caleb thought to himself how awkward the situation was. The General probably knew most of what he had been doing in Boardland, their special powers, along with the names of all the leaders in each city who were going to help them. If he captured the leaders and their key followers in each town that would more than likely keep the rest of the drawings from fighting against him. He also had his sisters locked up. However, from what the Little General was saying, he may want to trade. Caleb tossed his pack back into the closet. When he closed the door he heard a faint, "Let me out of here!"

As he looked over at Mr. Abe he could see he was shaking his head back and forth as he rubbed his beard. "This is a peculiar situation. I never would have imagined a standoff like this. Needless to say, I imagine this changes any plans you have for ridding Boardland of the General and his Fingers."

Caleb also had been thinking, "Not at all. It just complicates things a little. However, I don't understand why he hasn't already captured or smudged the leaders we talked to. He did leave Sketchard and a few others from Abstractshire and Primitiveville partly smudged on the trail leading into the Forest of Memories as a warning."

"I believe the General is doing the same thing you're doing."

"You mean gathering information and developing a plan?" Caleb replied.

Mr. Abe smiled. "I told you he wasn't a fool. He knew the Legend and even though he acted like he didn't believe it, he didn't even let his Fingers know all he was up to. He wanted to understand his adversaries, the Talbots, before he acted."

Now Caleb seemed more determined than ever. "Okay, so he knows just about everything. There is one thing he doesn't know and that may be the key to his demise."

"I thought you had carried the Little General with you everywhere?" Mr. Abe asked.

"Except as I said, when we were home in the Forest of Memories and talked about arming the drawings with erasers and when we were alone in Zephyr's office where we drew and created hundreds of erasers which we secretly sent to three cites."

Finally, Mr. Abe's frown disappeared. "So you've armed our citizens with erasers with which to fight the General and his Fingers?"

"The erasers haven't been passed out yet, due to spies, but when the time is right Coal, Sketchard, and Zephyr will do so."

"Looks to me like you do have a plan and it's already underway."

"It's a plan in progress and I think it's about time to make it happen," Caleb replied.

"Then how can I help?"

"Actually, the last piece of the puzzle rests with the drawings of Realtown. I need to know if we can count on any of them to help."

"I knew it would come down to Realtown some day. As with any ruling tyrant, those who benefit most from his rule will not want to see his rule end. I know it's shortsighted and selfish, even when they know others, probably all the Scribbles and Scrawls of Abstractshire will be erased, but drawings, just like real people, often look after themselves first. There are a few who understand that even if they now benefit, a land without freedom and equality, a land where a tyrant harms his own citizens, is a land where even they can be treated unjustly at any moment. All of Realtown knows of your arrival. Most are afraid of what you might do to ruin their selfish world. They know their artistic qualities will keep them safe. Yet, there are a few who are ready to help. Just tell us what to do and we will."

"That will help a lot," Caleb replied. "The last thing I need to know is exactly how many Fingers the General has in his army. By what we've seen there are about two hundred, although with Swoop having one for lunch every once in a while, the number may be lower."

"I'd say you're right. Years ago, when they all suddenly began to appear, we counted three hundred. But the General's brutal disciplinary techniques and artistic standards erased some...and yes, Swoop did rid us of many," Mr. Abe replied. "You must remember that the General's most effective weapon is himself. He can smudge and erase drawings in seconds."

"That's why I have to devise a way to separate him from the main battle," Caleb replied. "I need to put my plan in motion as soon as possible and I really want to free my sisters. As I recall, Monday is the day the General said he'd attack and erase Abstractshire. I have to assume that's what he intends to do. That leaves me with the rest of today and Sunday to put my plans into action."

"Then what do you intend to do, save your sisters?"

"Of course, however, they'll have to wait till Monday morning during Recess. I'll ask Swoop to fly me over the Castle walls and drop me into the General's patio garden. I can't fly and land on a small spot like that without getting hurt. I'll work my way to the dungeon while his Fingers are sleeping and free everyone. Swoop can then fly me out to where the main group of drawings are waiting with their erasers in hand to surprise the General when he leads his troops to erase Abstractshire."

"Aren't you afraid he'll attack Abstractshire before Recess?" asked Mr. Abe.

"That's a chance we'll have to take. I'm assuming he'll call his troops together and start out towards Abstractshire, but he won't want to attack until after Recess. If he hasn't erased everyone and everything before Recess takes place, his Fingers will fall asleep in the middle of battle, making it possible for me to erase them. Besides, the drawings helping us would also be at risk since the General doesn't need to sleep during Recess."

"I see what you mean."

Suddenly, a startled Spring appeared. "Mr. Abe, Caleb!" she yelled out. "While I was outside watching for Fingers, I spotted Curly hiding in the trees behind the house."

"I guess that pretty much proves he's a spy," moaned Mr. Abe. "I'm really sorry about that. Sounds like you'd better leave before a group of Fingers come for you."

"No, No!" Spring exclaimed. "I snuck up behind him and grabbed him. He didn't fight or anything. He just said he needed to talk to Mr. Abe and Caleb, and that he's sorry for what he has done."

Mr. Abe looked across the room towards the back door. "Is he waiting outside?"

"Yes, in the trees just behind the swing," Spring replied as she bounced towards the door.

"This could be a trick to get us outside," Caleb cautioned. "The General probably knows we're here since the Little General is in your closet."

"Then, Spring, would you please show him in. Maybe we can trick him into telling us the General's plans," said Mr. Abe.

A moment later Curly came through the door and into the front room.

"I'm really ashamed of you, Curly," said Mr. Abe. "I trusted you as a friend and you betrayed us all."

"Yes, I did, and I'm sorry. I didn't want to spy but the General has had R and S in his dungeon for several months and said he'd erase them if I didn't cooperate. I can't let him do that! They're like my family! Now that he's captured Nadie and Carona and the Legend may die with them, I have to do something."

An unsympathetic Caleb replied, "What can you do for us? And why do you expect us to trust you?"

"You have every reason not to. But now I really want to spy against the General to help Boardland. Besides, I know that once he's erased Abstractshire, and all the drawings living there, he'll erase everyone in his dungeon, too. The only way to stop him is to beat him."

"I'm still not sure if you're telling us the truth, Curly," Mr. Abe replied.

"Then let me convince you. I want to help. Caleb, both you and Mr. Abe have only about fifteen minutes to run and hide before the General arrives with his Fingers. He knows you're here. I don't know how he knows but I heard him call his troops together just before I rushed over."

"Sounds like we'd better hurry!" Caleb exclaimed.

Mr. Abe paused for a moment, and then spoke.

"Caleb. You go on, I'll only slow you down or stop you from flying to safety. Besides, I've expected for some time that the General would tire of giving me a certain amount of respect for being one of the earliest drawings in Boardland. There is a place in Realtown where Mary and I will be safe. Spring knows where that is. When the time is right, let me know what you want us to do."

"I will do as you ask," Caleb replied. "Then Spring you better come with me."

"What can I do to help?" Curly asked.

Caleb, still not sure of Curly's allegiance, decided that a little misinformation for the General would be in order.

"Curly, if you really want to help, tell the General, or whoever shows up, that I and the other drawings are heading to Abstractshire to defend it from his upcoming attack. Then find out what he plans to do and tell Sketchard."

"I'd be honored to do that, Caleb. I only hope you'll come to trust me again."

Caleb picked up Spring, then grabbed his backpack from the closet and headed out the front door as he heard a muffled, "Hey, what are you doing?"

"Getting in a little flying time," he replied as he ran and jumped yelling "high in the sky", then lifted off the ground.

It was late in the afternoon as he sailed through a couple of clouds only to get some chalk in his eyes. "Higher! I need to get Flicker or Gleam's attention," he thought as he flew up as high as he could towards the Great Illuminator's bright, warm light. He didn't feel a wall or ceiling stopping him from flying up. However, he was beginning to worry as the light and heat became more uncomfortable with every minute he flew upward. He finally realized that if he flew any higher the Great Illuminator's heat could destroy him. Just as he decided to start down he heard a calm, soothing voice.

"Caleb, Caleb, you fly too close to the Great Illuminator. You must go down."

He was relieved to hear Gleam's concerned voice. "Gleam, I'm so glad you're here. I didn't know how else to find you or Flicker but to head to your source of power and light."

"You've done well. It was risky but we're both near now."

"You mean Flicker's here too?"

"I'm right below you, Caleb, how can we help?"

"You probably know that the General has Nadie and Carona locked in his dungeon while Mr. Abe has gone into hiding."

Gleam floating just above Caleb replied, "Of course, the Great Illuminator knows all that happens and shares what he feels is appropriate with us."

"Then he also knows that the time is right!"

Then you have a plan?" Flicker asked.

"Yes, but I'll need your assistance as well as the help of all the drawings who said they would fight for Boardland's freedom."

"We said we'd do whatever you asked," Gleam replied.

"Then please fly with me to the Forest of Memories and I will share my plans with you and how you can help. I can't tell you more until I'm able to place the Little General, who's in my backpack, in a nice warm closet."

Chapter Eleven

The Plan

Curly heard a loud crash as the General knocked down Mr. Abe's front door and sauntered into the living room followed by Captain Thumb.

"And what do we have here? A Scribble to erase?" he yelled as Curly began to feel his short legs weaken.

"Oh, Mr. General…I…" Curly tried to say.

"My General, no need to erase this Scribble, this is Curly Que, one of our best spies. I've told you about him and the information he's provided. Remember, we have his letter friends in your dungeon?" Captain Thumb quickly explained.

"Then he should be able to tell us where the Talbot boy and Mr. Abe are," he grunted out as Curly felt his body freeze with fear.

"They just left," he blurted out.

"Just left?" the General asked. "Then where did Mr. Abe go?"

"He said he had a secret hiding place somewhere."

"And where is that?" Captain Thumb asked.

Curly knew that question would follow but wasn't sure what he should say. "I, ah don't, ah...know, Mr. General. I...guess that's why he calls it a secret place."

"I thought you said he was one of our best spies. I feel like letting some chalk dust fly!"

Curly knew he'd better talk fast. "Caleb said he was going along with some drawings to Abstractshire to help them stop your attack!"

"Really," replied the General as he backed away from Curly.

"Then Caleb ran out the door and flew away," Curly quickly added.

"That I know. But I also know he's apparently changed his mind and is now heading to the Forest of Memories," the General offered as he twisted his long black mustache.

Captain Thumb looking puzzled asked, "My General, who told you that? None of our spies have reported."

"You fool, I know things that even our spies don't know. After all I am the ruler of Boardland. So, he plans to try and stop me from erasing Abstractshire, one Talbot all alone with a measly band of drawings to help him? I won't need more than half my army to smudge and erase this riffraff. Yet, maybe I'll take all of them. They could use a little more smudging practice before we smudge another city or two. Besides I don't want to be away from my castle for too long."

"Then I can go?" Curly asked.

"Yes, go and find the Talbot boy and let us know of his plans. You'd better be quick or we'll be missing the eighteenth and nineteenth letters of the alphabet!"

Curly ran as fast as he could through the opening that used to be the front door.

"And you, Captain, tell the men to search every house in Realtown. Mr. Abe couldn't have gone far. Have them do it nicely, after all these are the best drawings Boardland has to offer."

As Caleb landed at Nadie's house, Flicker and Gleam floated in next to him. When he put Spring down she began to wobble back and forth.

"Are you all right, Spring?"

"Just a little bit dizzy, I'm not used to flying. I'll be fine in a few minutes," she replied as she continued to wobble.

"I need to put my backpack away and then we can talk," Caleb explained as he ran into the house.

Within a moment's time Caleb was back with the map of Boardland and gathered the four of them on the front porch.

"So, what is your plan and what would you like us to do?" Flicker asked.

"Just about every drawing in Boardland who said they would help will be needed. We have one chance of beating the General and his Fingers and we must take them by surprise. I've learned that the General is no fool. He's very calculating and likes to manipulate everyone, even his own men. He always wants the center of attention and feels he deserves it. Like most despotic rulers he's egocentric and feels invincible, and therein lies his downfall. If we do take him by surprise and cause him just a moment of panic or doubt, he will become angry and frustrated and could act carelessly trying to regain his hold. Since he won't share all his plans with Captain Thumb, there will be no one to assist him when he acts irrationally."

"You have learned a lot about our adversary, Caleb," Gleam noted. "You've done well."

Caleb nodded then continued. "The General will want to carry out his plans on Monday and attack Abstractshire. Since he said he'll do it, he'll have to save face and show all the drawings he means what he says. He already knows that there'll be some drawings at Abstractshire willing to fight against him. He just doesn't realize how many there will be. Like all despots he has deluded himself into thinking that most of his subjects actually like him. On Monday morning he'll probably gather his Fingers on the road in front of his castle and then lead them through the long grassy meadow. He'll want to wait until mid morning after Recess before he marches his foot troops and cavalry to Abstractshire. He won't want to risk them getting erased by me when they fall asleep."

"So how are we going to stop him?" Spring asked.

Caleb paused, and then smiled, as he pointed to the castle on the map. "He'll never get a chance to march his troops more than a few hundred yards across the meadow area in front of his castle. We will attack him as soon as he starts to move. Actually, we will trap him and his Fingers before he knows what hit them. Because of his anger and arrogance, I hope to be able to lead him away from the main body of his army. The Talbots have a special treat for him. In the meantime, we have several of Boardland's leaders to contact and a lot of drawings to put into motion. So, here's what I'd like each of you to do."

Caleb spent the next two hours spelling out the intricacies of his plans. Spring, Gleam, and Flicker all agreed to do their parts on Sunday. Spring was to contact Curly and have him give misinformation to the General and pass on a message to Nadie and Carona. She would also find Mr. Abe and let him gather those drawings in Realtown who were not afraid to act. Gleam was to contact Swoop and the Great Illuminator for their assistance. Flicker was to put the drawings in Abstractshire, Primitivepality, and Impressionville in motion by contacting Sketchard, Coal, and Zephyr. He would also give a message from Caleb to Prism. Caleb would contact Groff and the Tunnelers on Sunday.

When Caleb had finished laying out his plans, Flicker actually began to make his light vibrate and flicker very fast. "We knew the Talbots would develop a plan to save Boardland!" he said in his excitement. "The time is right, the Legend is going to be fulfilled, and the..."

Before Flicker could finish, Spring, who had started bouncing as soon as Flicker began vibrating his light, erupted into song. "Finally, we'll be free. The Eraser is going to flee. The Fingers will follow, we'll be merry tomorrow, and all live happily!"

Caleb looked across at both of them, smiled and said, "All that will happen if everything goes as planned."

Sunday was a busy day for everyone. Spring found Curly in his home in Abstractshire. She told him to go and tell Captain Thumb some of the drawings were preparing to fight them while others decided to run into the forests and hide. He was also to say that Caleb was there to defend Abstractshire with a small group of drawings from Primitivepality and Impressionville, because most of their citizens had been too afraid to help. Then he was to get to the dungeon and tell Nadie and Carona that, during Recess on Monday, Caleb would rescue them and divulge the rest of the plan. Caleb felt he had no choice but to trust Curly, since he was the only one who could possibly get a message to Nadie and Carona.

After Curly had left, Spring hurried to Realtown to find Mr. Abe. He was to gather any willing drawings from Realtown before Recess on Sunday in the north side forest just outside of the General's castle.

Gleam didn't need to share Caleb's plans with the Great Illuminator since he already knew. He also knew how he and Gleam were supposed to help on Monday. Gleam found Swoop who reluctantly agreed to meet her and Caleb before Recess on Monday in the forest by the south side outer walls next to the castle.

Since Flicker was a Beam, he could travel anywhere almost instantly. First, he went to Abstractshire and told Sketchard to arm his citizens with the erasers in the secret bag. Then they were told to go before Recess to the east end of the long grassy meadow in front of the castle and hide in the trees where the road from the castle entered the forest. Coal, Mayor of Primitivepality, with his drawings also armed with erasers, was to hide down the road in the south side forest near the castle. Zephyr, the leader of Impressionville, and his eraser armed citizens were to join with Mr. Abe and the Realtown drawings in the north side forest. All were told to travel off the main roads to avoid being spotted by the General's patrols.

While at Impressionville, Flicker told Prism that Caleb wanted her to meet him in the meadow just below Indigo Mountain, shortly after Recess on Sunday. At first, she complained that she wanted to stay and fight with the citizens of Impressionville, but Flicker told her to have faith in Caleb, so she agreed.

Caleb spent part of Sunday in the tunnels just outside of the Forest of Memories looking for Groff and Satch. He finally found them near Rockbound Valley.

"Am I glad I found you!" he exclaimed as he ran up to Groff and Satch.

He apparently startled them since they both jumped back.

"Oh! It's Caleb!" Groff bleated out. "We're not used to seeing anyone in our tunnels...except you, over the last few days."

"Sorry I ran up on you like that. I've been looking for you for some time. I need your help on Monday morning to rid Boardland of the General."

Groff looked surprised. "Then you have a plan and you need our help?"

"Yes, you and your friends are actually the key to its success."

"Do you remember what I told you when you asked if you could use our tunnels?" Groff replied.

Caleb knew he needed to be diplomatic if he was to secure the Tunnelers' help. "Yes, you said I could use them in an emergency but that you didn't want to risk losing any more friends."

"I also said that the General didn't bother us as long as we stayed below in our tunnels."

"Yes, I remember. However, you have helped. You've become good friends to me and my sisters as well as to the drawings of Boardland. The drawings see you as friends and respect you for saving our lives."

"That is true, and we do appreciate being recognized by the other drawings," Groff replied.

"The part of my plan that you can help with allows you to stay in your tunnels. The drawings in each town will be risking their lives while you'll be relatively safe in your tunnels. I know that there are very few Tunnelers left, so this way your sacrifices will be small."

Groff turned to Satch and grunted, "Interesting," Satch nodded back.

"Then tell us just what you have in mind and we'll check with the council. We, too, would rather have the General and his Fingers no longer a part of Boardland. It would be good to spend some time in the sun once in a while without being threatened by a large eraser."

Caleb spent the next few minutes explaining how his plan worked and what they could do to help. His plan had the Tunnelers split into two groups. The largest group was to be in a tunnel under the meadow grass east of the castle. A smaller group was to be in the tunnel they had dug under Indigo Mountain where Caleb had first spotted a Tunneler. As Caleb shared his plans, both Groff and Satch became more interested. They even looked at each other and grunted several times, which seemed to indicate they liked what they were hearing.

"You have learned a lot about our land in such a short time," Groff noted. "We can understand why the Legend spoke of the Talbots. We will talk to our council. If they agree, by evening you will find a fresh tunnel opening in the bushes to the right of the trail that enters the Forest of Memories. It will lead directly to the castle."

"That will be fine. However, by then it will be difficult for me to adjust my plan if your council decides you won't assist."

"Caleb, you are a friend. Both Satch and I like your plan and feel it can work. We will recommend to the council that they participate in ridding Boardland of the General. You shall find a tunnel!"

"Captain Thumb!" the guard on duty called out.

The Captain opened the large door to the castle and peered out. "Yes?"

"That scribble, Curly, is at the gate. He says he has information for you and the General. Should I erase him?"

"No, No, I was expecting him. Send him to me."

"Yes sir!" the guard snapped back as he saluted. "I will bring him immediately!"

Curly felt himself shaking. He had only been in the castle two times before. The first was several months ago when he and R and S were captured and placed in the dungeon. At that time, he convinced Captain Thumb that he knew everything happening in Boardland and that if the Captain didn't erase the three of them, he would spy and bring back important information. If he did, the Captain said he would let R and S leave. Unfortunately, Curly had kept his part of the bargain while the Captain kept threatening to erase them if he didn't continue. The second time had been when he was reporting to the Captain and had been allowed to wait in the great hall while the Captain passed the information onto the General. Today he hoped to get in the Castle again and then run to the dungeon while the Captain contacted the General.

"So, you have some information for me, Curly?" the Captain asked.

"Yes, Captain, but it will take a moment to tell."

The Captain looked around outside and saw several Fingers in the large courtyard. He pulled the large door open and allowed Curly into the great hall.

"This better be good," Captain Thumb growled, "I'm not sure I should be letting you into the castle."

Curly knew what he must do but he still trembled with fear.

"Captain, I have news of some drawings led by Caleb Talbot who plan to stop you when you march on Abstractville tomorrow."

"That's to be expected," he replied, "but we'll far outnumber them. Now give me something useful!" he demanded.

"Most of the drawings don't want to fight the General and have run off to hide. Caleb's troops will be few."

"The General has more supporters than even he imagines. He will be pleased to hear this. Anything else?"

"Only that Caleb will be waiting with his drawings in the forest as you approach Abstractshire."

"Very good, Curly."

"Then you'll release R and S as you said you would?"

The Captains slight smile quickly turned to a frown. "Don't toy with me you miserable Scribble. No, that is not possible. After our victory tomorrow, the General himself may want to reward your services by doing so. As for now, I will allow you a brief visit to the dungeon while I pass on your information to the General."

The Captain signaled across the hall to a Finger who was guarding the steps that led to the dungeon. The Finger quickly ran over. "Let this Scribble into the dungeon, but only for a short visit with those Scribbles we have in the large cell."

The Finger gestured for Curly to follow him as the Captain moved across the hall to the spiral staircase. Curly followed the guard down into the dungeon where another guard stood watch. They talked for a moment then the dungeon guard pushed Curly towards the Scribbles who peered anxiously through the bars.

Curly looked to his right and saw Nadie, Carona, and Half Pint also watching. Near to where the guard had stood, he noticed the girls' backpacks and several erasers lined up along the wall. He moved closer to the bars where R and S stood. The guards moved away a few feet and began to talk.

"I only have a minute," he whispered. "Hopefully by tomorrow afternoon you will be free. But first I must talk to the Talbot girls. You need to distract the guards so I can talk to them."

"We will do it," R whispered back. "Until tomorrow," she replied as she turned and quietly mingled with the other scribbles.

Suddenly, a chorus of voices screamed out. "Curly don't go! Help us! Save us!" they yelled as they tore at the bars and jumped around screaming. The guards ran over startled and surprised.

"Stop your screaming!" they shouted and swung at the bars with the heavy batons they'd pulled from their waistbands. "You'll get us all in trouble!"

Curly quickly moved to the cells that held the girls.

"I have a message from Caleb."

"Yes, but first get us the chalk from our backpacks!" Nadie demanded.

Confused for a moment by Nadie's sudden request, Curly, stumbled toward the wall, looked, then reached into each of their packs and pulled out the chalk boxes. As he turned around, he noticed that the two guards were reaching between the bars hitting some of the Scribbles and knocking them to the ground. A cloud of chalk rose around them. Jumping back to Nadie he handed her the boxes. She stuffed them into her pocket as he said, "Tomorrow, during Recess, Caleb will come for you. After that he and most of Boardland will be attacking the General as he leaves to erase Abstractville."

"I'm taking an eraser to the lot of you!" one of the Fingers yelled as he turned and moved towards the wall while also seeing Curly near the girls. "And what do you think you're doing!" he yelled above the screaming.

"Just trying to stay out of your way, sir," Curly sputtered back.

As the Finger gabbed an eraser he exclaimed, "Then stand over by the stairs or I'll erase you too!"

When the Scribbles saw that Curly had moved away from the girls they stopped their screaming and moved as much as they possibly could away from the bars and huddled together. Two letters lay on the floor slightly bent out of form.

"You see what a little eraser can do, don't you, Scribbles?" the guard said as he reached in and pretended to erase in the air where they had stood. Now try that again, and we'll both come in with erasers and empty the cell. All that will be left of you is chalk dust, and that I'd be glad to sweep up!"

"Now you'd better get that Scribble Q out of here before I practice on him," the dungeon guard yelled at the other Finger. "And don't tell any of this to the Captain or we'll both be coughing chalk!"

Curly headed up the stairs well ahead of the guard.

"Stop right there," the Finger commanded as he appeared, "We'll wait for the Captain's return."

"A fight they want, a fight they'll get," laughed the General. "I may even have to wear a mask tomorrow to avoid choking on all the chalk dust that will be flying, and I'm used to it!"

"Yes, my General. It looks like Boardland will soon have more room for only the best drawings that appear."

"And that, Captain, is the whole idea! Especially after I clean out my dungeon and maybe even Primitivepality. Those drawings have always bothered me anyway. I just wish Room 7 was a college art class instead of those artistically challenged fourth graders!"

"And tomorrow, General, what are your orders?"

"Muster my horsemen and foot soldiers in front of the castle wall before recess so we can leave immediately when it is over. Leave a few to guard the castle. I want as many of my men as possible to overwhelm these upstarts tomorrow. They have to be taught a quick and final lesson! Besides why should I not let my men enjoy themselves, too? A brisk march through Boardland will be invigorating, along with a little chopping with swords and poking with spears, and of course the inevitable smudging and my erasing. It will be a very pleasant day for all of us."

"Should I send out patrols or consult our other spies?"

"And what could they say to change our day. I told all of Boardland I would erase Abstractshire on Monday, and that I will do no matter what. Besides, what are they going to do, hit us with sticks? Altogether, even with that Talbot boy, they're no match for us. And speaking of that Talbot boy, I look forward to putting him into my dungeon myself. I look at it as graciously allowing a family reunion!"

Chapter Twelve

The Battle

Caleb returned to Nadie's Forest of Memories house. He knew it would be a lonely night without Nadie and Carona and hoped they'd be all right until Monday morning. He laid down and carefully reviewed his plan. He didn't want to overlook anything. One mistake, one drawing not carrying through with his assignment, one miscalculation with the timing, and the plan would fall apart like a house of cards. What haunted Caleb the most was the part of the plan where he would distract the General from the battle and lure him away. If the General stayed to fight, many drawings would be erased and the battle could be lost. He'd be chased and hounded and even with his special powers, eventually, overpowered by sheer numbers and end up as a trophy, along with Nadie and Carona, in the General's dungeon.

Caleb was ready to close his eyes when a bright light appeared.

"Flicker?" he called out.

"Yes," Flicker replied, "I hope we didn't startle you."

"No, I was just about to get some rest. Wait, what do you mean, 'we'?" he asked. Then Caleb noticed another smaller beam of light.

"It's just me, Spark, Caleb."

As Flicker moved closer he said, "Spark came with me. He wants to help, too."

Caleb rubbed his eyes, "Of course, Spark, you can be my messenger during the battle. You could even sneak into the General's dungeon without being noticed and find out if Nadie and Carona got my message from Curly."

"Oh, I've already done that," Spark replied.

"You have?" a surprised Caleb asked.

"The Illuminator's smaller beams are seldom noticed since we usually only show ourselves for a brief moment."

"Then what did you find out?"

"Curly did give the misinformation to Captain Thumb and also passed on your message to your sisters. Oh, he also snuck them the chalk boxes from their backpacks."

"Wow, I guess he can be trusted. So, they have their chalk in the cell with them?"

"Yes, and as Carona watched the guard, Nadie began to draw on the back wall."

Caleb knew that if his sisters had their chalk, they would be better able to protect themselves.

"What did you see Nadie drawing?"

"I'm not sure since I dared not stay too long, but it looked like she was drawing pictures of erasers and even a large key."

Although Spark's report was a good one, Caleb became concerned. If Nadie and Carona tried to escape or were discovered to have erasers in their cell, it could make it difficult for him to carry out his rescue plan. The General might move them somewhere else in the castle or become so angry he would hurt them.

"I really appreciate your help, Spark, and I do have an important job for you, " Caleb said. He knew he needed his sisters to wait until he arrived. "Would you help protect my sisters tonight and during the battle tomorrow? And let them know that they should stay put until I come for them?"

"Of course," Spark replied. "I have never really liked the General from the day he first arrived... so pompous and arrogant. When he and his Fingers took over Boardland the Great Illuminator had to calm me down. He told me about the Legend and how the General would be forced out of Boardland someday soon. I've... we've, waited way too long for that to happen. I'll do anything you ask."

"Then we're glad to have your help," Caleb replied.

"As for all the messengers you sent out to everyone, the drawings know what they must do and all of them plan to be in place tomorrow," Flicker reported.

"I feel better already," sighed Caleb.

"Then we'll leave you so you can get some sleep," Flicker said as he and Spark disappeared.

Caleb woke up just as the Illuminator's light began to shine. He drew himself some breakfast and prepared for the chalky taste that accompanied each meal. He knew his first job was to confront the Little General and lead what he hoped would be a quick and successful battle. He took his backpack from the closet and placed it unopened on the table.

"So, you're finally going to let me out?" he heard the Little General ask.

"Nope, I like you best right where you are."

There was a brief pause before the Little General spoke.

"The General may want to place you in a cell, but when I'm free and you've been captured I'm going to put you in the smallest closet in the castle and seal it up, except for a small hole through which I'll occasionally push a little food. You'll spend years being as miserable as I am in this smelly pack!"

"First, you have to escape, and that's not going to happen. In fact, I'm going to wear my backpack with you in it when I protect Abstractshire today. So, if anything does happen to me, it will happen to you too."

"The General always knows where I am and he'll do anything to get me back unharmed. When he does, he'll tie you up like the main course at a barbecue."

"Complain all you want, but just to let you know, I have a very useful job planned for you and the General. Don't worry, I'll make sure you'll be together for a very long time."

"What are you talking about?" emerged the snarled words from the backpack.

"You'll see," Caleb replied then fastened on the backpack and headed out the door.

Caleb felt he needed to check on the movement and battle positioning of the drawings from each town. He realized that his appearance would give them more confidence. First, he needed a place to hide his backpack until the battle began. He didn't want the General to know what he was up to until the time was right. As he approached the forest that bordered the Northside of the road, he saw Zephyr and the drawings from Impressionville cautiously proceeding through the trees with the erasers, along with crude wooden lances, in hand. Further into the forest he found a large oak tree with a small rock formation near its base. There he hid his backpack. He knew that the tree was near the spot where he wanted to lead the General when the battle began.

After signaling Zephyr and his men, he moved nearer the castle and watched the General's foot soldiers and cavalry preparing for battle on the road in front of the castle wall. As expected, most were armed with lances and swords. First, they'd poke, slice, and then smudge the drawings. Next, the General would follow up erasing those who had been injured or stood in his way.

Caleb continued around to the far east end and observed Sketchard and his drawings hiding in the forest on both sides of the road. Abstractshire had the largest number of drawings so their surprise attack from the front should be impressive. He then moved around to the south side of the forest and quietly greeted Coal and the drawings from Primitivepality, who like Sketchard's men, carried erasers and long wooden clubs. Everyone seemed more at ease when they spotted Caleb. He finally moved to a position in the forest on the south side outer wall next to the castle and patiently waited for Swoop.

Recess would be upon them shortly, yet Swoop had not arrived. Caleb began to doubt he could succeed without his help. The small garden patio inside the castle was far too small for him to safely fly into, then run and jump into the sky. He must have Swoop's help putting him in and taking him straight up and out.

As Caleb waited, he moved through the bushes towards the front of the castle and saw the General's troops lined up on the road ready for the march on Abstractshire. The foot soldiers were already laying down preparing for their Recess nap while the cavalrymen were beginning to dismount from their horses. In the very front were Captain Thumb and the General. The General was mounted on his large and beautiful black stallion that must have been drawn by an art teacher. Looking very dignified in full uniform, the General kept prancing around his men checking out every last detail of their uniforms, and equipment. He would probably keep watch over them as they napped. So far, everything was working out the way Caleb had planned. He counted two hundred and ten Fingers, a few more than he'd expected. How many were left inside the castle walls he didn't know.

He moved back to the bushes along the castle's south side to anxiously wait for Swoop who by now was very late. Recess was nearly over by the time Caleb felt the wind and rising dust from Swoop's wings.

"Sorry I am late. I saw a Finger a-ways down the road going on patrol and thought he might see all those drawings sneaking through the woods."

"That was a very wise thing to do," Caleb replied.

"You mean to stop for a quick breakfast?" Swoop asked.

Caleb, not sure what to say, added, "Yes, ah, breakfast and that other thing. But now I need you to fly me over the castle and put me down in the patio garden. Then wait about fifteen minutes and pull me back out after I release Nadie and Carona from the dungeon."

"Oh, is that all. If I want to have a snack, can I pick off another Finger?" he asked.

"Yes of course, but wait until the battle begins. With you flying in and grabbing a snack, it will make all the General's soldiers feel, let's say, less confident."

As Swoop spread his wings, he picked up Caleb and flew over the top of the castle and lowered him down into the patio garden as easily as if he were a helicopter.

Caleb immediately ran to the garden door that entered into the main hall. He knew from his visit three days before that he'd need to get to the far side of the hall and into the large dining room before heading down the stairway to the dungeon. When he entered the dining room, two Fingers were at the large table slowly starting to sit up. Caleb didn't like to do it but he pulled the eraser he'd brought from his pocket and quickly erased them both. It felt strange since they appeared to have solid, yet chalky bodies. When touched by an eraser, they seemed to easily erase into dust. That must be why the General, a massive eraser, could erase so many drawings in a short period of time.

As he hurried down the stairs prepared to surprise and erase any Fingers who might be waking up, he almost knocked over Nadie as she was heading up, eraser in hand.

"Whoa!" a surprised Nadie yelled out. When she recognized Caleb, she quickly embraced him. "Caleb it is good to see you! Curly told us you would be coming and so did Spark. We just thought we'd meet you in the dining hall."

Right behind her was Carona who also gave Caleb a big hug.

"How'd you get out?" Caleb asked.

"Curly got our chalk for us," Carona replied, "and we drew erasers and a key that looked just like the cell key the Fingers had! It worked!"

As Carona finished, Caleb noticed that behind her the stairwell was filled with drawings with Half Pint in the lead.

"Half Pint, it's good to see you," Caleb exclaimed. "Let's all go into the dining hall."

Entering the dining hall, Caleb counted about twenty-five Scribbles carrying erasers, including R and S, Curly's family.

You've sure been busy with your chalk," he noted. "And R and S, Curly will be happy to see you."

"Caleb, all the erasers work! We just tested them on the two guards we surprised when we bolted from the cell," Nadie said proudly. "Now, what's the plan?"

Caleb summarized what was going to happen and told them that he had to leave with Swoop any minute to deal with the General. He also told them that they should attack the General's men from behind as his troops would soon start their march forward. The

General won't feel he needs a rear guard. For now, they should erase every Finger they could find inside the castle wall."

"Nadie and Carona, when the battle starts, without endangering yourselves, use your chalk to fix any chopped or smudged drawings. That way we'll continue to outnumber them and encourage the other drawings to keep fighting.

"We will! Now you'd better get going. We only have another minute or two to search the castle and get ready to attack," exclaimed Nadie.

"The time is now!" Caleb yelled as he ran through the great hall and out into the small patio garden where Swoop was grazing on the flowers.

Nadie and Carona split the Scribbles into several groups and sent them running around inside the castle to erase any Fingers they found. Then the two girls started out the door into the walled courtyard.

When they pushed open the door, they momentarily froze. Sitting in the gated entrance were two large contraptions they hadn't seen before harnessed to four horses. Nadie instantly pulled the door nearly shut as they both peered out. Fourteen Fingers were in the compound, two were apparently drivers sitting on top of each contraption. They were driving what looked a bit like large wagons with four wheels. Extending from each of the four wagon wheel hubs were long shafts with blades along them that would obviously rotate as they moved forward. Four

Fingers, holding long lances, were climbing into the back of each wagon. The last two Fingers in the courtyard were about to open the gate.

"Carona, we can't go out. If they know we're here the General may send his troops to attack us first. We need to warn Caleb. Those wagon things can grind up a lot of drawings once they get moving!"

Instantly, a bright light appeared behind them.

"May I help you?" Spark asked.

Both girls spun around with their erasers held high.

"Oh, Spark, it's you!" Nadie bleated out.

"Yes, it's just me. Caleb asked me to help you during the battle."

"You certainly know when to appear!" Carona noted.

Nadie regained her composure and asked, "Can you take a message to Caleb?"

"Certainly."

"Then let him know about these two strange horse drawn wagons that have long blades with which to cut up the drawings."

"I will tell him," Spark replied as he suddenly disappeared.

Caleb and Swoop had landed in the forest near Zephyr's men. The men had just awakened from Recess and were being joined by Mr. Abe along with approximately fifty drawings from Realtown. Zephyr was passing out his remaining erasers to some of them.

"Mr. Abe, it's good to see you," Caleb said as he walked over to shake his hand, "and I see you've brought some citizens from Realtown."

"Yes, these are the true believers in democracy, drawings who know that freedom from a tyrant can only be bought by risking all they have."

"I'm glad you've been able to join Zephyr and the citizens of Impressionville for it looks like Recess is over and the General will soon start his march."

"Caleb, Caleb," was suddenly heard as they all looked around and saw a small light beam.

"Spark, is everything all right with my sisters?"

"When Nadie and Carona started to enter the courtyard from the castle they spotted two strange wagon-like contraptions with long bladed rollers sticking out of their hubs. Each wagon was pulled by four horses having two drivers and four Fingers with long lances on them. Nadie wanted me to tell you."

"Thanks, Spark. That is good to know. It looks like the General does have something up his sleeve," Caleb replied.

"And that could be a game changer," Zephyr added. "Those things could cut up many drawings in just a few minutes!"

Having grown in just three days into a strong commander, Caleb replied, "No it won't. I believe we can stop them before that happens."

"How can we do that?" asked Mr. Abe.

"If the General knew he'd need them right away those wagons would be at the front of his troops, but he has no idea that we're going to attack him in front of his very own castle. Coming through his gates last, they won't be able to move forward when Sketchard and Abstractshire attack him from the front. Then even if they are able to move into position, or turn north or south when we attack from both sides, I believe Swoop's desire to hunt will serve us well."

"Swoop's desire to hunt?" Zephyr asked.

Swoop, who was resting near the spot where he'd dropped Caleb, looked up when he heard his name.

"Swoop," Caleb called out, "Do you want to hunt Fingers?"

Without looking too concerned, Swoop replied, "You already told me I could snack on a Finger once the battle begins."

"Would you like to snack on a couple of Fingers driving wagons, along with knocking a few others out of wagons?"

"Sure, but I don't think I could eat more than one. Remember, I've already had breakfast."

"Good, then as soon as you see the wagons charge forward, snack time is on me," Caleb replied.

Just then one of Zephyr's men appeared, "The General is starting to move his troops up the road!"

"Good, it's about time. Tell the men to get ready to charge," Zephyr replied.

Caleb, along with Zephyr and Mr. Abe, moved forward to the edge of the forest where they could observe the General and his stallion prancing ahead of his troops. He was followed by his Calvary made up of approximately seventy horsemen. They were followed by Captain Thumb and the foot soldiers with the strange wagons pulled just behind them.

Suddenly, a lot of yelling could be heard from down the road. It startled the horses causing the riders to rein them up in order to gain control. The General looked totally surprised.

"So, they want to be erased here! That's fine with me! Look, it's just a ragged bunch of Scribbles from Abstractshire. We'll all be back in the castle for lunch! Cavalry, prepare to charge!" the General yelled.

"Great!" Caleb exclaimed. "We've caught him off guard and he hasn't noticed the erasers they're carrying!"

Sketchard charged his drawings a few hundred feet towards the General as they yelled and swung their long clubs. Just as the General ordered his cavalry to charge, the Scribbles stopped. They watched as the seventy horsemen with lances pointing forward quickly began to close the distance between them.

"Hold your positions, men," Sketchard bravely commanded, although he knew they were all fearful, having never encountered such a situation.

The General looked down in dismay at the trench full of his cavalrymen.

Just as the cavalry was almost in reach, the earth between them and the Scribbles began to crumble. At that moment the brightest light the drawings of Boardland had ever seen flashed across the sky momentarily blinding the horsemen. A hundred yards long and twenty feet wide trench appeared. The trench reached from the edge of the north forest across the grassy meadow and road to the south forest. It happened so fast the cavalry men didn't have time to rein in their horses as man and beast disappeared with loud screams and thumps into the deep trench causing a huge cloud of chalk dust to explode into the sky. From the trenches could be heard the loud growls of the Tunnelers and more screams.

The General, who had charged part way with his cavalry, had now jumped off his stallion and was looking down in dismay at the trench full of his cavalrymen. Angrily, he jumped back onto his saddle still not quite believing what had happened to seventy mounted cavalrymen.

Sensing they had a chance at victory, Caleb, waved his arms as Zephyr from the north side, and Coal, from the south side, both yelled, "charge!"

Hundreds of drawings waving clubs and lances shot out from the forest. The General's stallion seemed to move in circles not knowing which way to run as the General froze in his saddle. Captain Thumb immediately ordered the wagons to the front. The

General seemed as though he wanted to retreat when he turned towards the castle gate only to see Nadie, Carona, Half Pint, and the twenty-five scribbles hurry through it carrying some of the General's own lances.

This was the opportunity Caleb had been waiting for. The General was no longer sure of himself, having the possible taste of defeat in his mouth. Caleb ran as fast as he could to the oak tree and pulled on his backpack, and then returned. He could hear the Little General yelling, "Don't take me into that mess, you hear me?"

As the drawings were almost upon the foot soldiers, Captain Thumb, ordered one wagon to charge to the north and the other to the south. When the drawings from Primitivepality and Impressionville saw the rotating blades coming towards them they immediately slowed their charge. They had not expected the blades and for a moment several began to turn towards the safety of the thick forest.

Suddenly, several sharp and piercing screeches could be heard as Swoop appeared diving from the sky at a speed none of the drawings had ever seen him fly before. Instantly, the two drivers of the wagon charging to the south were picked up and swung into the forest. On his second pass, the lance men in the back of the wagon charging north were thrown through the air. The two Fingers driving that wagon jumped from their seats and began to run back toward the castle. Swoop shot down again attacking the four lance men in the first wagon, knocking three of them onto the ground as he grabbed the fourth in his claws. He turned and made one more pass down towards Caleb where he screeched, "Thanks for the snack," and flew away.

The drawings immediately jumped forward. Many of the General's foot soldiers turned towards the castle and started to run and then slowed as they spotted Nadie, Carona, Half Pint, and the scribbles advancing towards them. The Captain began shouting orders to his men. The drawings were quickly upon the Fingers using their lances or clubs to block the lance thrusts and sword swings of their enemy. As the drawings moved in closer, they pulled out their erasers swinging them at their opponents.

Dust was flying everywhere. Nadie, Carona, and Half Pint, along with the scribbles, charged forward blocking the Fingers' escape. As soon as a drawing was cut or smudged, the girls quickly redrew it. Sketchard and the scribbles from Abstractshire worked their way around the giant tunnel cave-in caused by the Tunnelers and joined the battle.

By now the General noticed the erasers and was as speechless and totally disoriented as Caleb had hoped. Suddenly, his face turned red with anger. He began to shake in his saddle as though he was about to throw out a chalk dust storm.

Now the time is right, Caleb thought. He immediately pulled the Little General from his backpack and swung him around in the air. The Little General began to scream out all kind of threats as he yelled for the General to help him.

The General stopped shaking and looked over at Caleb with such a hateful expression that for a moment even Caleb felt vulnerable and threatened. Realizing he'd completely captured the General's attention, Caleb started running into the northern woods. Sure enough, the General left his Fingers and rode after him. Caleb knew the General was so distracted and angry he had completely forgotten to fight and erase to save his own troops.

However, Caleb now had this massive, angry and evil eraser charging right on his heels. He knew the General would have the fastest horse and that the fastest Finger horsemen had almost caught him. He needed the General to follow him. If he jumped into the sky to fly, the General might give up the chase. So, Caleb ran faster than he had ever run before. He saw in the distance the tall indigo mountain on which Carona had drawn another rainbow and cave two days before.

In his hand the Little General continued yelling and threatening him with all kinds of painful retribution. Above the yelling, he could hear the pounding hooves of the General's horse as it charged closer. Caleb prayed that everyone who was playing a role in the final part of his plan was ready.

Caleb ran past the lake and through the flowered meadow and then stopped just in front of Indigo Mountain. He was relieved to see that the rainbow and cave chalk marks Carona had drawn were still on the mountainside. Prism stepped out from behind the rocks that he, along with Nadie, Carona, and Flicker, had hid behind when they watched the parade upon their arrival in Boardland.

"Am I glad to see you!" Caleb exclaimed. "The General's almost across the meadow. Are you and Gleam ready?"

"Just as you asked," Prism replied as she moved over and stood directly between the Great Illuminator's rays and the mountain where the chalk rainbow was drawn.

"I'm here too, Caleb," the soft and angelic voice of Gleam shared. "I will focus the Illuminator's rays through Prism and onto the mountainside."

"I sure hope this works," Caleb exclaimed.

"I know it will," Flicker added, who with his long white hair and red eyes was floating just behind Caleb, "for the time is right!"

Caleb forced himself to hold his ground as the thundering hooves of the General's stallion slid to a stop in front of him causing a large cloud of chalk dust to rise. The General dismounted and started walking towards him. Caleb needed to look up in order to see his eyes.

"You have something that belongs to me! And how dare you invade my world and threaten my benevolent rule!"

"Benevolent rule? Why you're just a pompous, self-serving tyrant who somehow tricked himself into believing he was an art critic and should rule a land where he himself looks like a Scribble!" Caleb couldn't restrain himself from blurting out.

"You know so little of our world, child. You have no idea how much I'm revered and respected."

"Respected? When you erase and torment the drawings at will! When you send your Fingers out to smudge the art work created by others as though you know better than the artists what they were trying say?"

"Enough! Now give me the Little General before I take you back to my dungeon! I still have a village to erase!"

"I'm afraid, General, that your army of Fingers is no more. Actually, the last of them are presently floating over your head in that large cloud of chalk dust," Gleam noted.

"That can't be true and even if it is, it won't take me long to force others to take their place. No one wants to see their families erased!"

"How about your little look alike dolly," Caleb replied. He began to swing the Little General around his head as Gleam focused the Illuminator's light through Prism and onto the chalk rainbow. Instantly, the chalk rainbow turned into a brilliant rainbow at the same time as Carona's chalked tunnel opened on the mountainside.

Suddenly, the General plunged forward, grabbing Caleb by the head as Caleb launched the Little General into the tunnel. The Little General landed hard on the floor of the cave and screamed out for the General to help him.

"Not until I've taught this upstart a lesson he'll never forget," yelled the General as his gigantic hands closed around Caleb's neck. No matter how much strength he had in Boardland, Caleb realized he was no match for the General.

Unexpectedly, the General screamed when two large eagles, that seemed to come from nowhere, descended upon him tearing with both beak and claw. He immediately let go of Caleb and tried to fight them off with a sword he'd pulled from its sheath. Swinging wildly, he backed into the cave hoping they wouldn't follow.

Caleb instantly recognized the two raptors that only days before he'd drawn in the trees next to Nadie's house. Where they had been he didn't know, but right now they were trying to protect him from a massive eraser.

Instead of leaving, the eagles kept tearing at General Eraser causing him to back further into the cave. Finally, they ceased their attack and flew away. The General reached down, picked up the Little General, looked out through the bright rainbow-colored opening at Caleb, and yelled, "I'll make you pay for this!" He stumbled towards the tunnel opening with his sword in one hand and the Little General squirming in the other.

He'd only taken a couple of steps forward when the ground in front of him opened up and ten Tunnelers started biting at his legs and body. Bits of his eraser body began to shred off. Chalk dust commenced to obstruct Caleb's view as he saw the silhouette of the General running further into the tunnel. Then there was silence. Even the Tunnelers had swiftly disappeared into the ground.

Chapter Thirteen

Answers

Caleb stood looking at the mountainside as the rainbow's brilliant light began to fade then turn into sparkles that slid off the granite surface and onto the ground. The Tunnel was gone. He turned and looked at Gleam who simply smiled and winked at him, then dimmed her light and floated up towards the Great Illuminator. Close behind her was Flicker.

Prism walked over to Caleb and took his hand, "Thank you for all of Boardland. The Legend has truly been fulfilled."

All Caleb could say was, "Thank you, Prism."

Still he did not believe what had just happened. He did know one thing: he needed to get back to the castle and see how Nadie and Carona and everyone else had fared.

Caleb spotted the General's stallion standing patiently. "I don't know about you, Prism, but I'm exhausted. Would you like a ride back with me?"

Prism smiled and said, "I'd be proud to ride with you."

When they arrived back at the castle, Gleam had been right. There was not a Finger in sight. The two wagons sat alone on the large grassy meadow. Nadie and Carona were just finishing redrawing several of the injured drawings that had been chopped or smudged. The citizens from each of the towns in Boardland were shouting and celebrating together as they intermingled for the first time since the General began his rule. Caleb noticed a light in each drawing's eyes that he'd never seen before. He realized that they had hope and knew they actually had a future without the evil actions of a tyrant. Now all drawings could live together and be respected for the artistic intentions of their artist.

"Caleb!" Carona yelled as she ran over and embraced him. "Is the General gone?"

"Yes, he and the Little General disappeared into the rainbow tunnel you drew. I'm not sure where they are, but I know Boardland is now free of them."

"Then we did it!" Carona shouted as she hugged him again.

Nadie was hugging him, too, as she said, "Then I guess the time was right for us to have come and save Boardland. Everything happened just like the Legend said."

"That seems to be true, but I still don't know why we were picked and everyone knew our names?"

As the Talbots were talking, the citizens of Boardland gathered around them. Several drawings started chanting, "Talbots, Talbots, Talbots."

Soon, as everyone joined in, the sound became almost deafening. Some of the drawings from Realtown picked each one of them up and paraded them around to the rhythmic chanting. Caleb even spotted Curly Que in the crowd hand in hand with R and S. Nearby stood Mr. and Mrs. Abe along with Coal, Sketchart, and Prism.

In the distance he saw a Scribble, which he recognized as Spring, bouncing around the meadow singing. Soon many other drawings who were nearby changed their chorus and joined in with her.

As Caleb listened he heard, "Finally we are free. The Eraser in fact did flee. The Fingers all fell. The Legend we'll tell, and we'll all live happily!"

Soon everyone was chanting with her.

Finally, the three Talbots were put down as the chanting and singing faded. Everyone began to walk around patting each other on the back causing small whiffs of dust to appear. Caleb noted that Groff and Satch, along with about fifty Tunnelers had popped out of a nearby tunnel and had been chanting along with the rest of the drawings. He, Nadie and Carona hurried over to thank them. The festivities slowly waned as the drawings started to wonder what was going to happen next to Boardland now that the General and his Fingers were gone.

"Caleb, Nadie, Carona," they heard Mr. Abe say, "could we talk for a moment?" As they turned they were surprised to see Flicker, Gleam, and Prism standing with him.

"Sure, but first we want to thank all of you for your support and trust. We could not have done this without you and all the brave citizens of Boardland."

"We appreciate your humility, but as you know if we could have eliminated the General by ourselves there would never have been a need for you and the Legend," Mr. Abe replied. "Yet, as for Boardland, some of us have been talking and we all agree that our first choice for leadership would be the three of you. We're offering you the opportunity to rule as a Tribunal except you'd be held accountable to a council made up of leaders selected from each town."

"Kind of like a group of Presidents, with a legislative assembly to double check our decisions?" Caleb asked.

"That's exactly it. We want strong concerned leadership we can trust, along with the democratic ideals of elected representatives from all the drawings," he replied.

Caleb looked over at Carona and Nadie. They both seemed pleased that Boardland trusted them enough to ask them to help rule but neither seemed overly enthusiastic.

"You know, Caleb, even though things haven't gone well for us at home, it still is our home.

"He, Nadie and Carona hurried over to thank them."

Boardland belongs to the drawings, not to us," Nadia noted.

Carona, who had been listening intently added, "Nadie is right. The Legend never said anything about the Talbots staying, only that we would help them get rid of the General. As for me, I don't want to be in a position where I'd have to judge art or the artist's intent. I prefer to simply enjoy the imaginations and work of every artist!"

"Well, Mr. Abe," replied Caleb, "we appreciate your trust in us but we need to be getting back to our world. Boardland had problems, but in our world, we need a lot of creative and mature problem solvers. I think when we get back we'll see things quite differently and be better able to contribute to helping our world do the right thing for all its citizens."

"We thought you'd probably see things that way," replied Mr. Abe. "You were our first choice, but as a backup, the leaders of the other towns voted for me to serve as President and asked me to develop a quick plan for electing representation from each town for a representative assembly to balance out my executive power."

"I think that's a great idea!" Carona exclaimed.

"Then that's what the three Talbots would like to see in Boardland," Caleb added. "I have to admit, I know you'd be a great President!"

"Thank you. I will do my best to serve every drawing," Mr. Abe replied.

"So, Mr. President, we do have some questions," Caleb mentioned.

Mr. Abe looked around at Flicker, Gleam, and Prism then back at Caleb. "Then what would you like to know?"

Carona quickly spoke up, "Is the time now right for us to travel home?"

"Of course," Gleam replied. "The Legend has been fulfilled and you still have your chalk along with Prism and the Great Illuminator. I believe you may leave whenever you wish and we'll all do our part to see you return safely."

"Then we'd like to leave as soon as possible," Nadie shared. "But first, how did you know we were part of the Legend, and how did you know when the time was right?"

"Ahh," sighed Flicker. "That was something I wasn't allowed to share with you until, let's say, the time was right. So, now I can tell you. We have known about the movement of drawings into Boardland from Room 7 since the beginning. We were aware that the Creators were the teachers who have taught in that room along with special art teachers and others who wrote on the blackboard. We also realized when Abstractshire grew so fast it was because the majority of artwork and written work was that of the fourth graders who were assigned to Room 7."

"But how did you know someone from the real world could travel through the blackboard and even go back with you?" Nadie asked.

"We didn't until one late afternoon. Manny, the school custodian, was cleaning the room and began singing his favorite song, "Over the Rainbow". He happened to have some colored chalk that he'd found in his custodial closet and decided to draw a rainbow on the blackboard. Suddenly, the setting sun's rays passed through the prism hanging near the window and the tunnel you saw opened up. Needless to say, Manny was very surprised. I just happened to be traveling through Boardland when I noticed this tunnel appear from where the drawings always seemed to enter Boardland in the early mornings. So, I stopped and peeked in."

"Then Flicker, you discovered the tunnel link between the real word and Boardland?" Carona asked.

"I guess I did, but I was even more surprised when I went into the tunnel and saw Manny looking back at me from Room 7."

"Did he travel to Boardland too?" Caleb asked.

"No, just the three of you have. But Manny and I talked several times after that and he promised not to tell anyone about the tunnel. Then one day your father came to visit him at Sutter Heights Elementary School. Your father, David, had formed a strong relationship with Manny as a student there. Over the